The Incredible
Life of
Willie Sharp

VMH Publishing
Atlanta

The Incredible Life of Willie Sharp

Robert Thurston Hankins, Jr.

To My Lovely Wife, Sharon Hankins
My Children:
Robert, Johnell, Raheem Zamiel, Raziyah
My Elders
Regina Hankins, Garry Williamson, Claudia Nervis
Muata Rasuli, and the Oliver Family
The Winston Family
To The Loving Memory of
Thirston Thomas Hankins
Robert Thurston Hankins Sr.
Robert Williamson
Edward Winston
Sonny Ballard
James Mitchell
Elliott Johnson
And Wendell Stuart

"This is the moment of truth. The moment we create in our minds, here is the time to make manifest our dreams and our goals. At this moment, we will decide how we are remembered. warriors, wizards, kings, or be not remembered at all..." – Raheem.

CONTENTS

Chapters

1.

Thursday, January 30th, 1986 was the day that my life made an unsuspecting turn into the world of thaumaturgy. It was an unusually cold winter afternoon in Oakland, California. The air was sharp; it whipped around my 12-year-old cheeks as I hurried home from school. The sky was clear like polished blue glass, as the sun beamed down, sparkling like a diamond, which made the bitter sting of the cold breeze seem puzzling. I thought to myself, *how could the sun be so bright, but the earth so cold at the same time?* I walked down the streets on Oakland's northside in a neighborhood known as "Short Shattuck." It was called that because of the row of dead-end streets that began at 46th and ended on 49th Shattuck Avenue. I walked past a neighborhood bar called the 'Birdcage', the sounds of bobby blue bland pouring out the door, oozing onto the concrete outside its guarded doors. I'd always slow down to soak in the syrupy sounds that teased my eardrums so sweetly. Yeah, man, inside the birdcage is where I wanted to be.

"Sup Lil Brotha?" A deep, raspy voice broke the melodic meditation I was in... "What's sup lil man, what's hat'nin?" Super Willy, the Birdcage's bouncer, bellowed again... "you headed home to get that schoolwork done, huh?"

I replied, "Yeah, Super, I gotta get my mind right, so I don't end up like your black ass!" Super then yelled, "What the fuck, you lil bumpy head bastard; get outta here!" We both laughed. I said, "Alright, Super, I'm out."

"Later, lil man," he said with a giant grin. I was back on my way home. It was crowded on the block this afternoon; the men were circling the block, picking and choosing women who'd stand there, swirling and swaying their hips, horns blowing double-time to attract someone willing enough to go home with them. I was getting closer to my home on 556 48th St. - my home since I was six years old. I passed the vacant post office parking lot, where the junkies hung in huddled groups, nodding to the battery-operated FM radio that blared. Each were taking turns to speak muttered words, because it felt so good. Across the street stood more women, showing off their scantily-clad bodies. My eyes seemed to get lost as they wandered in their direction. Men continued to cruise around, perusing the aisle of meat, trying to take their pick. I walked past the cars, most of the windows fogged up, hazily permitting me to see a muddled outline of intertwined bodies. Headed home I thought to myself, *man I can't wait to get back, I think my mom made chili,* which was my favorite food. I'd sprinkle a mountain of cheese on it with a glob of sour cream and go to town. Sometimes I'd eat so much of it I'd be on the toilet all night...but it was worth it; yep, I loved chili. This is what I thought about as I made these nightly walks. Finally, I got to the corner of my dead-end street, right by the old dentist's office turned boys' club, where all the kids from Short Shattuck came to hangout. Walking past, I notice a one-hundred-dollar bill on the ground; my eyes lit up with excitement. "Holy crap!" I shouted, looking around to see if anybody was watching. Nobody seemed to notice me or the money, so I went to pick it up when I heard a voice say, "Ain't nothing free in this world, but God." I jumped back so far that I fell onto the ground. *Who said that?* There wasn't anyone close to me. But as I looked up, I saw him - a tall black man, whom I had never seen before around here.

I wondered where he came from; it was like he just appeared out of nowhere. He leaned against the wall of the boys' club, staring at me with the type of grin that you only get when you receive a gift at Christmas. His clothes were neat and clean, with no lint or wrinkles. His suit had colorful, elaborate African designs. I know because I once saw it on TV - they call it "kinte." His grin showed a bottom row of sparkling gold teeth, and his hair was cut in a weird symmetrical pattern, like a sideways bicycle ramp. He wore shades where the tint gradually faded from the top of the lenses to the bottom... I also noticed the sparkle from the diamonds embedded at each corner of the rim. His sharp and chiseled facial features were square and exact; his high cheekbones reminded me of Chuka Zulu. His goatee was perfect as if God himself was his personal barber. His shoes were neatly stitched, with ostrich feathers. He proceeded to say again in a deep rumbling voice, "Ain't nothing free in this world, but God." A thin line of light appeared out the corner of my eye. I heard a low whistle getting louder, and then so loud it broke my gaze just in time to see a car screeching towards me, the driver trying frantically to stop. I embraced for the death blow, but it never came. Moments later I opened my eyes, and I was standing on the corner. I looked around but the man was gone; there was no car, not even skid marks from the tires. *What just happened? Am I dead?* I thought to myself, *where's the car, and who the hell was that dude? Was I daydreaming?* I sat there for a while, staring into the distance, confused. I thought, *maybe I'm going crazy.* It was getting late. I needed to hurry up and get home - I had to get to that chili.

The next morning, I woke up earlier than usual; I just couldn't stop thinking about what had happened yesterday. *Was it a dream? But how could it have been when it seemed so real?* I could smell the delicious bacon my mother was frying up; the sizzling and popping sounds got my mouth watering. I got up and saw what my mom had laid out for me, a striped burgundy and grey sweater with 'blue tough' skinny jeans and my blue pro wings tennis shoes. Damn, I hated those shoes, but my mom said it was all she could afford at the time, and besides, she said I went to school to learn, not to impress nobody. I did my routine of using the bathroom, washing up and brushing my teeth, getting dressed, eating my breakfast, and walking to school. But today was different; I walked outside in the cold air with a feeling that something was going to happen.

Walking up 48th, I saw two people arguing. When I got closer, I could hear that it was a woman, cursing a man out about not paying. I passed by and listened to her yell, "Ain't nothing free in this world, but God." It's like someone had hit me with a bat straight across the back of the head! I turned around. They stared at me like they saw a ghost. I stood there looking at them - they were frozen like statues. But I quickly realized they weren't looking at me; their gaze was fixed on something behind me. Then I saw it was him - the man from yesterday. I could feel it. I turned slowly to see him staring at the two of them, as if he was a God sent to judge them on the spot. The woman said, "I'm sorry, Willie. This mutha fucka is trying to leave without paying!" The white man looked like he was gonna crumple on the ground as he plead his case, saying shakily, "Come on Mr. Sharp; I would never do that to a lady! It's just that I didn't get what I asked for!" The man was silent...the white guy reached in his pants pocket and pulled out a roll of one hundred dollar bills and grabbed the women's hand, shoving the money into it. "See Mr. Sharp? No harm, no foul, right?" Mr. Sharp looked over to the white man's car, still not speaking a word.

The white man ran over to his car, jumped in, and before the engine could start right, he smashed into traffic up 48th headed towards Berkeley. The woman smiled at the man, winked, and said, "thanks, Willie." She then turned toward me and said, "you too, sugar," and began to strut down Shattuck, hips swaying from side to side. I turned to see the man walking into Birdcage. *Wow, so he was real; I wonder where he's from? Couldn't be from around here; I'd have seen him before. Well, whoever he is and wherever he's from, he's a cold mutha fucka,* I said to myself as I continued walking to school. Once at school, I told all my friends about the man, whom they seemed to know about and called "Willie Sharp." When class let out for the day, I couldn't wait to hit the block to catch a glimpse of this dude again. However, I didn't see him when I got to Short Shattuck. I said to myself, "oh well, maybe tomorrow I can hang with him at the birdcage." I laughed at the thought as I headed home.

2.

"Don't blame me, you created this world."
- Willie Sharp

Quite some time had passed, and I had not seen the strange man. I wondered where he went, and it seemed as if he had disappeared into thin air yet again. I asked the local players who hung in the neighborhood, but no one had seen him. Some didn't even know who I was talking about; I just chalked that up to them being lame and not deep enough into the streets to know a man of that caliber. Anyway, my life was changing. I was now becoming the target of the neighborhood bullies who were looking to find fresh meat to terrorize, and I just happened to fit the description. One day while in class, my friend was approached by a smaller kid who kicked him in the leg. My friend laughed it off, and the smaller kid ran back to a group of older kids who I recognized as a gang called "The Shittaz." The reason for this odd name was because if you got caught by the gang and didn't comply with their orders, they'd beat the runny crap out of you. It was a frightening thought to be lying on the ground with your pants messed up, so nobody dared to mess with them.

When the little dude who had kicked my friend told his gang what happened, I guess they weren't satisfied with my friend's reaction. I could read the lips of the leader when he said, "okay, now go kick the other one." My heart stopped as they all looked at me, the leader grinning as if he was a lion closing in on his prey. I was scared to death. I was already about to shit myself, so one good punch, and it was over for me. I thought to run, but it was too late; the kid had gotten within kicking range and was projecting his foot in a way that ensured my demise. I embraced for impact, flinching, but it never landed. In a fit of unconscious bravery and Bruce Lee rerun- tomfoolery I jumped up, and Kung-Fu kicked the crap outta this kid. I landed a thunderous, lightning-fast roundhouse kick to the kid's face so hard, that my foot went inside his mouth. The kid fell back several feet. Everyone, including me, was stunned at the attack I unleashed on this kid. But it was no time to feel sorry for that mutha fucka, I had to get outta there with the quickness...

I started running real fast, digging up the tiles and concrete from the cafeteria floor. All I could hear was the gang yelling something I couldn't quite make out. I hopped over fences into backyards trying to ditch the gang. Still, they were on my ass, and when I saw the laundry mat back door open, I ran in through the back and out to where the customers were washing their clothes. I knocked over a few baskets of clothes trying to get to safety, but the gang kept coming. I finally lost them by the freeway on 51st and Shattuck; there was an old trail that got you from 51st to 54th, and Grove St. I circled back to 45th, came up to Shattuck by the McDonald's fast-food spot and then to 48th - home at last. I told my mother what had happened and she became terrified. She talked about the kids these days having nothing better to do than to pick on other kids; I had failed to mention that I almost severed that six-year-old's head from his tiny body with my Kung-Fu skills. But, I figured she didn't need to hear the gory details anyway. The next day, however, the principal and the little kid's parents felt it necessary to tell her as well as show her picture of the carnage I inflicted on this poor kid. After explaining my side of the story, I got off with just a three-day suspension, and an ass whooping from my mom, which compared to ten kids beating the actual crap out of you, was pretty light. Besides, three days of relaxation ain't bad at all - forget school and them shittaz!

3.

"Who you are; who are you?"

Thursday morning and still no school; however, momma had gotten up to fix breakfast as usual. I got up, went to use the bathroom like every morning, and grabbed my washcloth to get the crust out of my eyes. I turned the hot water knob and waited for the water to get warm, testing it every other moment, and when it was hot enough, I placed the washcloth under it, squeezing the cloth and pretending that it was made of iron and I was the Incredible Hulk bending it to my will. Once it was full of steaming hot water, I made sure it was evenly hot; I placed the cloth to my face instantly, feeling the hot steam excavating the pores of my skin. I always held the cloth and kept it on my face until it began to get cold; that's when I'd start the process over. By the third time I'd begin to wash my face, scrubbing every inch of my face and neck. As I did so, I thought of Willie, wondering what his morning regiment was. I thought to myself, *he probably smoked a joint while brushing his gold teeth, then he probably counted his money with his left hand while brushing his hair with the right.* Yeah, something magical and cool like that. As I removed the cloth from my face, I was suddenly startled at the reflection in the mirror. I fell backward into the tub. I had seen Willie's gold-toothed face grinning in the mirror... there I was breathing heavy, scared, and confused at the image; it seemed so real. After a minute I was able to gain some composure and pull myself out of the tub to my feet. Afraid to look in the mirror again, I threw my washcloth in the sink and left the bathroom.

I joined my mother in the kitchen. I moved slowly to the chair, where I sat quietly, still shook from the hallucination that I had just experienced. My mother turned towards me and saw that something was wrong."Boy. you okay? Looks like you saw a ghost or something." I

I whispered, "I'm fine." Momma served some turkey bacon and eggs with two pieces of toast on the side. The savory smell wafted up to my nostrils, like the thick smoke that danced from old men's pipes. I shoveled down the food like a starved prisoner devouring his last meal. Once finished, I went to the living room, the rain pattering lightly on the windows. Momma had gone to the bathroom, and I had sat on the couch to find some good "mind control programming" on TV. 20 minutes later, the phone rang, interrupting JJ Evans proclaiming his title as "Kid Dyn-o-mite." The phone's piercing ring drew my attention away from the training video. I picked up the receiver and said, "chello?" doing my best to mimic JJ's voice. The person on the other line simply said, "let me speak with your mother." I replied to the voice, "she's in the bathroom," to which the voice responded, "Baby, never tell anybody your mother's personal business." She continued, "tell her to call Candy when she's available."

"Yes, ma'am." I hung up the phone and went to relay the message. I knocked on the door and told my mother what the lady had said...I heard the toilet flush, then the water running from the sink. The door opened. My mother said in a low tone while nodding in the affirmative, "okay, cool." She then went to the phone and began to dial. A minute went by, and my mother greeted the person on the other side of the line saying, "Greetings, Mother." I listened confused. After all, I knew that she hadn't called my grandma because my Grandma lived in Detroit, and she didn't dial enough numbers to make a long-distance call. So, who was she talking to? My mother listened intensely, nodding as if the person could see her agreeing to whatever was being said. After about 20 minutes of my mother's "uh-huhs" and "yes ma'ams," she finally hung up the phone. She sat for a minute as if she were replaying the words of the conversation in her head. She stared off into the nothingness of space, nodding and grinning ever so slightly. I wondered what she had heard and what would happen next.

I went to my room where I opened the window just wide enough to feel the cold breeze that rushed under the window sill, like water from a cracked dam bursting into my room, the warm air being wrestled and twisted upwards in an invisible fight for dominance. I always liked the feeling of the warm and cold air occupying the same space; it was encapsulating and invigorating. I seemed to be in two different realms of reality - one hot and one cold. I concentrated on the window as the tapping of the rain began to hit even harder. Yes, there was something about the shady grey clouds, the rhythmic sounds, and soothing touch of the brisk and simultaneously warm airs that I found quite enjoyable. I focused on the chipping paint the rainwater had softened as it ran down the sides of my bedroom wall; it was pretty to me - every drop made its way to a new world traveling from the sea to the sky then to my window sill. A voice suddenly called out, barely audible, competing with the boom-bap of the rain beating down. It called out again, this time louder and more aggressive....

"RAHEEM!" RAHEEM, BOY, DON'T YOU HEAR ME CALLING YOU?" I snapped out of my daze and answered my mother, who was standing in my bedroom doorway. "Huh?" I honestly hadn't heard her calling me. She said, "boy, we gonna have to get yo ears checked; I been screamin' your name for 45 minutes! I started to smack you to see if you were alive." We both laughed. She told me to get my coat; that we were going to visit someone important. She said that I could pick out my outfit, but that I had to hurry up because the person was expecting us, and she didn't want to keep them waiting. I went into my closet and picked my best outfit. It was some Levi 501's jeans, a pair of black penny loafers, and a multicolored rayon shirt. I also picked out a black apple hat that my grandfather had given me when I visited him in Detroit I showed my mother my ensemble. She grinned in approval, gave me my coat, and ushered me to the car. And just like that, we were on our way.

We took the streets. My mom was afraid to drive on the freeway; it always seemed strange to me because everyone drove fast on the freeway, so it seemed everybody was driving slowly, just moving fast as a group. But anyhow, we took the streets, first down Shattuck which then turned into telegraph after 45th St. We rode all the way downtown, past Molars Barber College, where most of the barbers at 'Macknificents' got their licenses from, on past the California Highway Patrol Station down the street to the bakery on 37th. After a few blocks of riding in silence, my mother reached for the big silver knob that controlled the radio, and I heard a loud click and then the soulful chords of Kool and Gangs' "It's Too Hot" oozing into the car. I didn't know what the lead singer was singing about, but I knew it was serious and cold-blooded, that it was too hot for him to stick around. *Wow,* I thought, as the vibrations seemed to dance on my skin. I closed my eyes and let the vibes flow through; I moved my head to the beats, catching the snare in time. I listened for deeper rhythms and found them in the hi-hats and bass guitar. Momma and I were grooving on down the street, clapping and snapping our fingers and having a good ole time. We jammed all the way down Telegraph Avenue and up E14th on our way to East Oakland.

4.

"See ya later, kid."

Once inside the old house, I could tell that this wasn't just any ordinary East Oakland house in the ghetto; the main entrance was marked by these giant double doors that had tall pillars on each side, with the earth on one and what looked like the universe on the other. There were golden leaves and fruit of some kind carved at the top just under the globes. The pillars must have been at least 35 feet tall, and I had a strong urge to climb them. The ceiling was painted to look like the night sky, with stars and planets and different solar systems too. As we walked the stars twinkled, and I almost fell a few times trying to watch the fake sky and keep up with my mother and the old women at the same time. There was a hallway in the middle of adjacent staircases that wound up to the second floor. We walked down the hallway; it was filled with old paintings of black individuals, donning odd-looking clothes. Some had crowns, while others wore a red hat that looked like the thimble from the monopoly

29

game; it had a long black tail that hung from the top of the hat. I stared at it for a long time. The old woman observed me while I gawked at the painting and different sculptures. There were many rooms, and they all housed some sort of treasure. Some of the rooms were filled with gold statues of men, women, and even children. Some of the rooms had ones of animals made from materials that glowed in the dark.

We finally came to a large room that had one single chair, and bright red pillows large enough to fit three or four people each covering the floor. The old woman motioned for us to remove our shoes; I was hesitant because I had put on my lucky socks which large holes at the top of them so that my big toes poked out of them, so I thought quick and pulled my shoes and socks off at the same time, rolling my socks up in my shoes so no one would see. We stepped onto the pillows, and it felt as if we were walking on clouds; as I walked closer towards the chair, which sat atop these shiny gold steps, I noticed how it had all kinds of diamonds and stones engraved in it. The old woman pointed and said, "sit there, Raheem." Hence, I walked up the three large steps and climbed up into the chair, the cushion enveloping me from the sides as I sank deep into it. "Comfortable?" the old woman asked. I replied, "yes ma'am," leaning back. "Good," she said as she and my mother walked over to a cabinet that contained little brass colored drinking cups. The old woman grabbed a tray with a kettle on it and brought it to the floor where she and my mother sat down. I noticed that the tray sat right on a pillow but didn't tip over as she poured the contents of the kettle into the little cups. Out of it flowed a light brown liquid, and in seconds its aroma filled the entire room with the sweet smell of vanilla and cinnamon. The scent was thick and intoxicating, and I began to feel even more relaxed in the chair.

The old woman reached under one of the pillows and grabbed a remote, and upon hitting the button she brought down a screen that had the local T.V. station playing. It was covering the news of a breaking story about an old comedian and actor who had been accused of doing bad things over 30 years ago and although there was never any proof, the media had made it look like he was guilty. The old woman said, "Raheem, never believe anything you see on the news, baby." The old woman then changed the channel. Now it displayed a blind man talking about the history of Africans; he talked slowly and was sometimes boring to listen to, but I was too busy trying to eavesdrop on my mother and the old woman to pay attention anyway. My mother asked the old woman, "mother dear, have you seen him?" The woman nodded.

"Where can I find him?" my mother asked in a low, frustrated tone. "I've got to find him; it's time, it's time." The old woman wrote something down on a small piece of paper she pulled from an inside pocket under her robe, and handed it to my mother. My mother read the note; it was an address. I knew because my mother had a habit of moving her lips when she read in her mind. I wondered whose address it could have been, but just then the old woman asked me if I'd like to hear a story. I just sat back in the chair and nodded yes.

She began her tale in Africa, over a hundred thousand years ago, talking about a people called "The Great RahSan." These people ruled the earth for millions of years. They had come from a different planet in a faraway galaxy, and she said that these people were said to be created from the stars by God Himself. They were loving and caring people, and there was no war, no disease, and no negativity. Most of them stood an average of seven feet tall, and their skin was so dark it seemed to glow with the outline of the Sun's rays surrounding them. These people lived off the Sun; it fed them and taught them how to replenish themselves after a great number of their powers were used. The Sun, as well as many other stars, taught them how to build great cities using only the material of the earth that could be used to produce electricity and transportation. The RahSan communicated with their minds and used an ancient dialect that sounded like what singing is known as today. They were also led by a council called the "Usda-pinea," who were the elders of the RahSan people; San's are said to have each been one thousand years old; however, they resembled the typical teenagers of today. The old woman talked about the great catastrophe. A Great Scientist named "Hsub" created a material to create other planets. Now in this time, the earth was alone in this solar system, just the great "San," which was the name for the Sun and the Earth which rotated around it. One day while testing his device, Hsub was electrocuted and hurt very badly. He was brought to the council where the members tried to use their powers to heal the great scientist, but to no avail. He had been stripped of his powers to communicate with the San, and his skin began to turn pale.

After months of resting in his home, Hsub thought he'd go to the inner city to get some magic fruit; he thought, *this could restore my skin*, but instead of taking his transportation machine, he felt that a good walk would help him feel better. He walked down the road, which was teeming with all kinds of vibrant flowers and lush greenery, but to Hsub, something felt strange, as he hadn't heard the birds or the animals of the forest. Only the winds blew harshly; the wind was pushing him away, and the more he walked, the more the wind howled. Hsub felt cold and wanted to turn back; however, he continued through to the inner city. He then came across some children playing in a park. He waved to the children, but they screamed and ran away. Hsub was shocked by this and wondered what could have prompted such a reaction, and he stood there perplexed. However, he was reminded of his mission to get to the fruit, so he continued.

Hsub noticed that the people who passed him on the road looked at him oddly. Some covered their eyes, and some children would begin to cry. Hsub started to walk faster as a crowd began to assemble, and someone yelled "wotso-tisit" which meant "what is it?" in the ancient RahSan dialect. Hsub started to run as the crowd chased him through the inner city, but by the time Hsub had made it to the fruit shop, news had spread that an alien had come and was trying to hurt the children. Everywhere he went, the RahSan were there yelling at Hsub. They had cornered Hsub into an alleyway and began to close in on him. Hsub pleaded to the crowd with his mind, but no one had heard him, because his communication powers had been taken by the electric shock of his machine. The group stepped closer, and Hsub stepped back. Hsub eventually stumbled backward and fell, catching his reflection in a piece of metallic material from a transporter. Hsub couldn't believe what he saw; it was a face he didn't recognize, with eyes that weren't his own. Hsub jumped back from the reflection, crawling back, trying to escape the hideous sight of the hideous creature he had seen.

Hsub started breathing rapidly and cried out, realizing the creature was him. He had lost all the hue in his skin. There was nothing left but a colorless, grey-pink derma. Hsub sobbed loudly as the RahSan carted him away to see the council. He was held in a big box with just enough room to stand up in; he could touch each side with his hands without fully stretching his arms, with only a skylight at the top as his source of air.

While there, the San's light emitted through the cracks of the box. Hsub looked up, weeping to the San, trying to communicate desperately with the great one. He asked, "why have I been mistreated so? What error did I commit? Why won't you talk to me?" But the great San could not hear him. Hsub was awakened by the rumbling of his box; he was being moved, and yet again he yelled "waya tak oma" to ask the RanSan what was going on, but his question was met with silence. Once he arrived at the destination, he looked through the hole at the top of his box and realized it was the council's chambers he had visited often to display his inventions. The box was set down and began to dissolve like fog on a hillside in the early morning. The council was quiet. Silence filled the room as the mumbling and whispers faded. They were speaking to one another with their minds. But Hsub couldn't hear them. Finally, after what would have been hours to us, the deafening silence was broken. The council had believed that the Great San had cursed Hsub

for trying to make planets because the great San
was the only one who could do so.

5.

The Rest of the Legend

The great San is angry with you and has shown us all that can happen when we behave as though we are like him. Yes, we are made from his being, we must never take on his role as the creator of things beyond our mental and bodily capabilities. You broke San's law, and now you must be brought to equilibrium with your ways," said the leader of the council. "I'm going to banish you from all our parts of the earth, and you may live wherever the RanSan people do not. Hsub cried out, "but I am RanSan too! I may look different, but I'm the same as you." "SILENCE!" the leader of the council thundered. "You are no longer one of us, as the great San has made you something else entirely."

"But, but...." Hsub pleaded. He was cut off by the wave of the council leader's hand. "Raheem, RAHEEM!" the old woman yelled, snatching me back from the story. "Are you keeping up with the story, child?"

"Yes ma'am," I replied, "this is an excellent story." This story was far better than the ones my mother would tell me. The old woman leaned in and whispered with a slight grin on her wrinkled face, "do you want to hear the rest?"

"Um hmm," I said, getting comfortable for the next ride into my imagination. The old woman took a long, deep breath and continued.

Hsub was led far from the lands of the RahSan to the northern part of the earth, where it was icy and lonely. Everything was white as far as the eye could see - the trees were white as snow, the animals and few flowers that lived there were all a pale color, and thick clouds blanketed the sky so as to never let the great San enter. Hsub wept for days, longing to go back to his people. He wandered around the cold, frigid terrain aimlessly. He heard a voice say, "no matter how much you cry, they won't let you come back." Hsub jumped up ten feet in the air. "Who said that?" He wondered if San had forgiven him, or if he would get his powers back soon. Then he heard laughing, and Hsub stopped in his tracks as a young girl appeared from a cave opening. "You're funny," she said. "What's your name?"

The sight of the girl frightened Hsub; she was pure white, blending in with the landscape so well that he couldn't tell where the snow ended, and her skin began. She said, "Don't be afraid, my name is Rakka. What's yours?"

Hsub stared for a while, making sure the girl was real, before replying, "I am called Hsub. I am RahSan."

The little laughed loudly, grabbing her stomach and falling forward to the snow-covered ground. Hsub, feeling angered by her laughter, shouted, "what is your problem, why do you laugh at me so?"

"Because fool," the little girl shouted back, "look at you, you're not RahSan, you are Nashar!"

Hsub was boiling mad now. "Nashar? You foolish little girl! There's no such people; you've been out here too long." Out of curiosity, he continued. "How did you get here anyway? How did a young girl like you get banned anyhow?"

"Banned?" the girl asked with a confused look on her face. "I was born here."

"Born here? That means that your mother and father are here too! Take me to them."

The girl hissed like a cat preparing to maul an enemy. Hsub, startled, asked, "what is the problem, did Isay something wrong?"

The little girl giggled and said, "no, I just like to make that noise sometimes. Come on, let me take you to our village." Hsub breathed a sigh of relief.

They had walked for a few miles when suddenly a voice called out. It was a language that Hsub didn't recognize, but he could tell the noise uttered was an alarm of some sort. There was quiet, and then the snow all around them began to move in from side to side in a swaying manner, left to right and back again. It was like a wave of white foam being agitated ever so slightly; some parts moving up and down. Hsub started to feel lightheaded as if he had drunk too much yennh wine. His mind reeling, his knees shivered and weakened with every motion of the snow. Its pace quickened. Hsub could no longer resist and began to sway in unison. He felt a spot inside his chest grow cold. Grabbing his stomach, he screamed with pain. He felt a small ice-cold needle in his gut, injecting frozen lumps of poison into him.

"Please stop, spar me this agony!" Hsub cried out while now rolling back and forth, up and down to the rhythm of the snow. The little girl was nowhere to be found. Hsub lay there, the pain gone, replaced by a tickle that was just as irritable as the frozen needle. Hsub closed his eyes for a moment, but was jolted upright instantly.

Hsub woke slowly to the warmth of something being rubbed on his forehead. When he opened his eyes, he realized it was the little girl rubbing a cube of ice on his face. He enjoyed the sensation of the ice cube's tingling touch. He thought, *how could an ice cube yield this type of soothing heat?* "What is this - what type of magic can make what is supposed to be cold feel warm?"

The little girl was confused by his question, as she had no concept of warmth, coming from a place where she only knew cold and ice... the old woman stopped the story to explain she had no idea of what warmth was. "In the land of the Nashar, all that is known is made up of ice, and their bodies don't feel like we do." The woman went back to the story. Hsub started to feel better, and as the days passed, he grew stronger and was able to help around the village. In time he became well respected and had assumed a powerful position among the Nashar people. Weeks turned to months, months turned to years, and in time Hsub became the leader of the village and sought out to make an alliance with the other Nashar people, soon forming one nation under the ideology of superiority over the lands. The Nashar had been far removed from the RanSan people and had forgotten of their relations or how their forefathers had been banished to this barely inhabitable part of the world. Hsub elaborated on the RanSan's cruelty, in which he had to embellish on. He created a story that would scare and then infuriate the Nashar...he said the Nashar were the original rulers of the earth and that they were overrun by the RanSan, and over half their population was killed or enslaved, but the most valiant warriors were banished and the Nashar were the offspring of those mighty warriors. Hsub told the people, who now believed him to be a prophet, that "it was ordained by the god of the Nashar that this was the generation that would overthrow the RanSan once and for all."

After years of training, Hsub had amassed a sizable army of warriors, so he gathered his generals and devised a plan to attack the RanSan people. And when the time came, he and his army made their move...but he always led first with people under the guise of wanting peace. They brought gifts, most of which had been stolen from the previous villages who were slaughtered as offerings, and when the RanSan villages let their guard down the armies would soon rush in, killing all the men and enslaving the women and children...this was done over and over again until the last of RanSan were all but wiped from the planet.

Just then, I was jilted from the movie in my mind as the old woman reached down to grab my cheeks, and she stared deep into my eyes. Her own eyes flickered like the flames of a roaring forest fire as she whispered slowly, "they killed everyone except us."

I screamed and yanked away from her, running through the house and out the front door to my mother's car; I jumped in and locked the door. I couldn't shake the feeling that I was going to be killed. After a while had passed my mother appeared outside with the old woman; they stood at the top of the porch, hugged, and said their goodbyes. My mother turned and walked down the steps while the old woman just stared at me and smiled. I smiled back - *it was just a story,* I told myself, and I waved goodbye. My mother and I drove off.

6.

How did we get here? How do we get out?

I remember riding down the street, headed home from that lady's house. I thought about all the fascinating artwork and sculptures in all those rooms... most of them had to be ancient. I thought about the sweet-smelling tea she and my mother drank and thought about the weird story she told me. I wonder what she meant by "just because it's the end of the legend doesn't mean it's the end of the story." That sentence played repeatedly in my mind. I was sure it was a riddle of some kind and that I had to figure it out. As the mustang moved smoothly through the Oakland landscape, we passed rundown buildings and faces scurrying in and out of the alleys that lay between them. The scent of despair was prevalent among the surrounding atmosphere. How could this exist underneath God's beautiful sky? The poor man's constant illusion of having something he thinks he owns, the wealth disparity, the inequality... the addicts in this neighborhood never look up, for their god is buried deep the pocket of a 15-

year-old child who randomly spits his blessing to the depraved dope fiend dying a slow hot funky death doing the "dopers dance" with the devil. *How did we get here?* I asked myself. *And how do we get out?*

Mom and I finally made it home. Exhausted, I carried myself up the front porch into the house and immediately flopped on the bed like a sack of wet clothes. I was out like the lights in a blind man's house. The next day was the last day of my suspension and my mother was going to take me somewhere. I thought, *hopefully it's another interesting old person, like the old woman from yesterday.* My mother had woken me up and instead of having my clothes set out for me, as she usually did, she let me pick my outfit. I was excited about that because, you know, I knew what was cool and stylish. My mother didn't grasp the 'concepts' I had in mind. I always felt a deep cool when I thought of myself and was able to execute my preferences. The older people, like my mom's friends, would say that I had an "old soul." I liked the 50's, 60's, 70's and early 80's style. In true fashion, I pulled out my finest ensemble, thinking whoever we were going to see today was going to be totally impressed. I had some cologne that my friend's dad had given me. I splashed it on my face and rubbed the rest into my clothes to get the sweet scent in there. When I was ready, I went into the living room where my mother had been waiting patiently. When she saw me she smiled with pride; I was looking pretty fly and as sharp as I could be.

We left the house on our way to see this person my mom had been so anxious to find. We eventually got to a section of Oakland off Broadway Terrace, where all the well-to-do people lived. We drove past the golf course lined with giant houses and fancy cars parked in front of them, past elegantly manicured lawns that had bushes trimmed into little animal figures. There was no trash, no dope fiends or women flagging men. This place was like a dream, a paradise adjacent to the nightmare that was merely kept separate by that invisible (but still obviously impactful) socioeconomic barrier. Yes, this place screamed "off-limits," especially for black people, but most especially, *poor* black people.

After some time we came to a parking lot that was occupied by more exotic, flashy cars and formally dressed people, some of whom were black! I made eye contact with a tall, very slender black woman with long flowing dreadlocks that swayed in the air, like magic vines controlled by an invisible puppeteer. She smiled and slowly made a gesture with her hands. I felt an inviting feeling as if the lady welcomed me, without words. My mother found a parking spot and pulled in. She took a long, deep breath and turned to me and said, "Be good, baby."

I replied, "Okay, I will." My stomach was now fluttering violently, as if a million butterflies were swarming inside, desperate to get out. I grabbed the handle of the car door and pulled; I could hear the chattering of happy people greeting one another. Some laughed gently as they embraced in a chorus line of hugs and kisses. The men smiled and shook hands and even hugged as well. There were hundreds of different types of people, of all races and from different cities around the Bay Area, gathered in this one place. The vibe was bright and loving, the overall mood infectious. My mother and I made our way to the sanctuary, which was a wooden villa that had been built by hand. It had large stained-glass windows, one of which had a giant symbol that looked like the letter V with two equal signs on its sides. This place was a makeshift library and cafeteria of sorts, that had a stage where plays could be performed; it also had a second floor for classrooms. After looking around the large facility, my mother and I sat on a bench outside. the sun was beaming down, and I instantly thought about the story the old woman told me about the RanSan and how they absorbed the Great San's rays. I imagined that the hair on my head was spreading apart and that the sun's light infiltrated my skin, illuminating me with a warm glow. My eyes closed and suddenly I was startled by a bell and people shuffling into the sanctuary. My mother grabbed my hand and led me through the large double doors that opened into a long hallway. The walls were covered in a gold metallic paint. I reached out to touch them, the texture feeling smooth and cold. I thought my fingers had sunk into the wall as I walked. The floor was covered with thick, deep, blood-red carpet that my feet sank into with every step, and it stretched all the way to the front, where a stage with a large glass podium was placed. A few feet behind it, there were three large throne-like chairs, each engraved with the 'V' symbol that I had seen in the stained glass window. I watched as all the people found their seats in the rows of comfortable benches that encircled the stage area, and noticed the instruments off to the far left of the stage, where musicians began tuning, before playing ever so gently. This gave the room a warm, soft, and melodic feeling, casting everything into slow motion. Mother and I had sat in the middle, close to the inner aisle. I looked down at the front and noticed an older lady looking over her shoulder at me.

Isn't that the old woman from yesterday? I thought excitedly to myself, *what was she doing here?* I waved at her, and she waved back before nudging a man with her elbow, who was sitting next to her. The man turned slowly, his eyes sparkling like sapphires as he grinned, showing his glistening gold tooth. I recognized him instantly - the man in the street. It was Willy Sharp. He nodded at me. I was so stunned I couldn't move; he looked at my mother, and they stared at one another for what seemed like forever. Something peculiar happened - my mother nodded as if she was answering a question that no one had asked, Willie look back down at me and nodded affirmatively, I heard the word "yes" and I turned to see who said it, but my mom was silent, and no one was talking to me. I looked back, and Willie was gone yet again. The old woman gestured to my mother and me to come to the front row where she was, so my mother ushered me down. Five minutes later, the music stopped. The lights were dimmed, and three hooded people with long white robes walked out in complete silence. It was eerily quiet, almost void of sound, and all I could hear was the air that swooshed around my ears, which somehow mimicked the waves of the San Francisco Bay crashing in slow motion against the rocks of the shore. With each soundless step the three figures took, I inhaled deeply until the three figures had sat down. When I looked up, I was surprised that even though the lights had been dimmed, the sanctuary was filled with a brightness that reflected on all surfaces, casting a kaleidoscope of color all around. The three figures removed their hoods, revealing women with long silver dreadlocks. I recognized one of them as the same women I saw in the parking lot when momma and I first arrived.

Just then I felt a tap on my shoulder. It was Willie. I had forgotten that he disappeared earlier; he then motioned for me to scoot over as he slid down between my momma and me. I stared at him, as I didn't understand what was happening. I had so many unanswered questions. Why was the old woman here? And how did she know Willie? And how did Willie know my mother?

One of the women on stage made her way to the podium and began prayer. Everyone bowed their heads and repeated after her. Then, she returned to her seat. The woman who sat in the middle chair arose and seemed to float to the podium, greeting the crowd before proceeding to talk. She talked about all sorts of unusual things, things that I didn't understand and sometimes I swore she said in other languages. She spoke about the power of love and that when one was ready to allow pure love to overtake them, then they'd be able to accomplish magical feats. She would meet eyes with all the people in the room, and each time she connected with someone, there seemed to be a tether, and a slight glow that covered the two of them. Her conversation and instructions went from the most intricate and complex thoughts down to ultra-simplistic ideas of life and the omnipotent. She explained that love is the ultimate form of which everything else was but a subdued reflection. We all listened intently until the service/ceremony was complete. We all shuffled to the courtyard where handshakes and hugs were exchanged, accompanied by deep insight (or befuddlement) into the lecture that just occurred. My mother and I found a place off to the side of the cafeteria, where we sat on a marble bench. The surrounding chatter began to settle into a low murmur of inaudible hums, and I felt my body sway to their rhythm. Then I heard a whisper..."Hey Youngsta, I see ya cashin' in on that God thang." It was Willie. He and the old woman had come to sit with my mom and me. He looked at my mother, she looked back at him, and not breaking eye contact, she said to me, "Baby, why don't you go and explore the church?"

"Yay!" I replied. I looked back over at them; they were in deep conversation, saying very few words but continuously gazing wide-eyed at each other. At one point, they stood up, formed a triangle, grabbed hands, and started to pray. I watched as they began to mumble something simultaneously, and as I walked further away the silhouette of their figures slowly blurred, like looking at a mirage from a distance on a hot day. On our way home momma told me Willie was going to teach me things. She said these things would help me on a mission I must take. It all sounded pretty vague, none the less it was excited.

7.

Supreme eye? What is that?

The next morning, I leap up out of my bed, running to the bathroom to brush my teeth, then I zipped back to my room to get dressed. I was bursting with excitement - I was going to hang out with Willie Sharp. He had said he would teach me things that would make a man. I laced up my shoes and grabbed my book bag, blazing out of the house I didn't even kiss my mother bye. I had to hurry to school to tell all the kids that I was going to learn the Game. In my mind, I was going to learn how to be a player, something I had dreamed of becoming when I got older. Willie was a master, and it wasn't hard to tell. The top hustlers around 48th Street all knew him and bragged about his abilities to make dreams come true. I made it to school and saw my friends huddled up in a circle in the cafeteria, and when I rolled up, everybody yelled and jumped around like I was Haile Selassie visiting Jamaica for the very first time. Just then, I had remembered the ass-kicking I laid on that kid last week. My friends were swinging their legs in a karate-kicking motion, mimicking the severe blow I delivered to this kid's skull. I was proud that I was the center of attention; however, I had something way better to tell them.

I slowly walked over to the nearest table with a strut. The crowd quieted down to a low murmur. I said, "ya'll wanna hear something super fresh?"

"What?" a kid named Morris asked. I leaned back and tilted to the left, crossed my right foot over my left knee, like the old men in the park I'd see, and said, "I'm going to be a wizard." The crowd was completely silent before erupting with laughter, as if I was Eddie Murphy in "Raw." I could feel myself losing my cool, my grin faltering. I was trying to keep it together, but the embarrassment over my statement was becoming evident.

The little kid I beat up the previous day shouted, "Did ya'll hear this fool? He said he's gon' be a damn wizard!" Everywhere I looked people were laughing, some so hard they cried tears, while others rolled on the floor. Even the janitor and lunch ladies were doubled over. I didn't know what to do. Before I knew it, I did it again - the poor kid didn't even see it coming. My left hand came crashing down out of heaven into this kid's eye, and he subsequently dropped like a sack of potatoes. Everyone around me was stunned, and once again, I took off running. This time, I didn't run home. I went to find Willie. I found him at the pool hall in the back of the birdcage bar. When I got there, he was in the middle of a shot, leaning over the table in a shooter's stance, concentrating like a cobra about to pounce on its unsuspecting prey. He drew back his cue stick, mimicking an archer pulling back his bow, and with a tense jerk, he took his shot, and SMACK! The cue ball thrust forward in a swift, calculated motion, crashing violently into the striped nine-ball, which ricocheted off the left side into the solid three-ball, going back and forth and side to side across the velvety green before falling into the corner pocket. Willie, in his signature low tone, muttered, "Game, mutha fuckaz." He threw his stick on the table, simultaneously spinning around on his heels to swipe up the large stack of one-hundred-dollar bills waiting for him. He licked his thumb to get more grip on the bills as he counted them one by one. Just then he froze in mid-count, his eyes darting toward me, his look of satisfaction morphing into a twisted look of disgust. "Who let this boy in here?" he asked around him.

The entire hall fell silent; the waitress who was at the front, startled, dropped her glass of alcohol, the glass shattering on the floor. Willie repeated himself, this time more aggressively. "I SAID, 'WHO THE FUCK LET THIS GOD DAMN KID IN THIS POOLHALL?'"

The waitress nervously motioned to pick up the broken glass, sheepishly replying, "I, I... I'm sorry, Willie... it was me." Willie glared icily at the woman for what seemed like an eternity. Everyone in the bar held their breath. "Bitch, you're fired," he said coolly.

The waitress burst out crying, and attempted to plead her case but was quickly cut off by Willie's finger, which pointed to the exit. At this moment, I was afraid and confused. The crowd had relaxed back into hustler's mode after she left, the jukebox blaring Johnnie Taylor's "Disco Lady" over the crack of the pool balls at the tables that lined the hall. Willie walked over to me, grabbing my shirt and lifting me off my feet. He dragged me to the alleyway on the side of the hall, the vile scent of piss and vomit permeating the air. Willie pushed me, and I stumbled forward a few feet before I could regain my balance. I turned around to see Willie lighting up a joint; I knew it was a joint because momma's friend "Garry Lue" smoked them every time she and momma would be getting ready to go to the club. At that time I never understood smoking something that smelled like a skunk's ass, but I caught on later in life.

Willie took a deep drag off the perfectly rolled joint and said, "see ya kid," before blowing the smoke upwards toward the sky. I followed the smoke as it danced to the distant music that lingered from the hall, before dissipating. Before I knew it, Willie was gone, slamming the door to the bar shut and leaving me behind, in the piss-soaked alleyway. I turned to go home and noticed my feet were sliding around some, and I looked down to discover I had stepped in a big pile of dog crap. And judging by the size of it, it wasn't from no dog, either. *Great.*

I went to Bushrod park up the street from 48th so I could use the bathroom to try and get the human feces off my shoes. After a half-hour of scrubbing, I was able to get most of the smell out and some of the stains. I wandered around North Oakland until I figured school had let out. When I reached the corner of 48th and Shattuck I had felt as if someone was watching me. I turned and saw that it was Willie. At that moment it began to lightly sprinkle. Willie flashed his lights and waved me over. He cracked the window ever so slightly, just enough to be able to utter the words, "come on man git in!" I climbed in, and we sat in silence for about two minutes before he said, "this is your first lesson, regarding the law of stillness.

"You must understand that the less you move mentally, the more you become aware of your inner vision. Now don't get this mixed up with being lazy, see, that ain't what's happening here. No, not at all. It's the calming of the mind and body, ya dig? It's allowing your true self to bubble up to the surface so that you can see with the supreme eye."

Supreme eye? What was that? I thought to myself as Willie talked, his words sweet and flowing like honey, but sharp like a bee sting. His words were enlightening yet mystifying at the same time, my body enveloped in conflicting sensations. As I sank into a hypnotic state my body began to buzz like I was gently hugged a swarm of tiny bees my heart slowed to a frightening pace, I was floating the more willy talked the more I separated from my body, I could see the light trail from his fingertips and balls of energy blast from the palms of his hands, time seemed to begin to stretch everything moved slower and slower and slower until it all just stopped my entire life froze, everything the birds in mid-flight, the trees that blew in the wind, the dogs who were running behind their masters, and the master himself, the car that zipped by where now in suspended animation as if God had reached down to earth and pressed pause on the material world, the raindrops that had exploded on the windshield and had burst into a billion separate expressions of a single drip seized like little Crystals shimmering in the headlights of the oncoming cars deprived of motion. It had all been arrested and taken into the custody of my mind. My attention was drawn back to willy, he had stopped talking and was staring off into the distance he sat there with his back almost vertical his diamond-encrusted hand resting on knees, like the old Egyptian statues I had seen in my school books he inhaled very slowly the air making the sound like the rattle of a venomous cobra he said did you see it? His eyes still facing forward, squinting as if he was piercing the veil of the universe. After some time I answered, "yes." "That was the supreme eye. It allows you to exist in the complete now." Willie continued "You'll need it to complete this mission." At that point I asked "what exactly is my mission?"

He just grinned and said, "there's nothing free in this world but God." That sentence echoed off the windshields and roof of the car, sending chills down my spine. Then Willie abruptly said, "see ya later, kid."

What was going on? What just happened? Little did I know I was a student, and Willie Sharp was my teacher.

8.

Inside me, something grows.

That week I went to school as usual. The days seemed to merge together, like cells from an old movie reel. Before I knew it, Sunday had shown up, and momma and I were off to church. Once we were on the road, I stared out the window. I remembered the euphoric effect Willie's words had on me. I tried to reenact the feeling, but no such luck.

After a quiet 20-minute ride, we arrived at a church called 'The Center for Spiritual Living." I had found out a couple of years later that this church was the first of its kind in this area and only a special kind of people attended. Since this was my second time here, I decided I'd give the teen church a try. I wanted to meet the other young people that I had seen the last time I was here and try to make some new friends. As it grew close to eleven o'clock, the crowd of church-goers began to gather in the main sanctuary. I went to the building and up to the second floor where the classrooms were. I saw a lot of kids, from very young kids to teens. Of course, I considered myself a teenager. I wanted to attend with the older, more 'mature' kids. However, I was just 12, which meant I was only able to attend the preteen class. It was taught by a man named Kwame, and he was a very interesting person. He had this way of speaking in a capitulating tone; even if you disagreed with what he was saying you had to surrender to the possibility of what he was saying. His way of teaching was comprised of a well-crafted sermon including both personal experience *as well as* spiritual truths, that were absorbed instantly by everyone in the classroom. Today we learned about consciousness. Mr. Kwame posed a question to the class, and everyone raised their hands except for me. I was new and didn't want to speak in front of the other kids. Mr. Kwame looked over the class, and his eyes seemed to zero in on me slowly, like a plane coming in for landing. I thought to myself, *No, no, don't pick me!* Butterflies were doing the soul train in my stomach. Once he fixed his gaze on me, he grinned slightly and said, "Hey little brother, what's your name?"

I froze; I couldn't speak properly so I mumbled something that somewhat resembled my name. He replied, "stand up, little brother, give us some good stuff about consciousness."

I rose hesitantly, and all the other kids were staring at me waiting for me to say something. The longer I stood there, the bigger Mr. Kwame's smile became and the less the butterflies danced. I finally said, "to me, consciousness is being awake as opposed to being asleep."

One of the kids in the class let out a sound of agreement followed by a "yep, yep; that's what I was gon' say, too." The other kids all nodded with approval. The young girls who had sat at the front of the class in a group began to whisper and grin at me.

Mr. Kwame said, "alright little brother, that's one way to explain it."

As I sat down, a chubby kid with dreadlocks stuck out his fist to give me a pound and said, "right on bro." I felt like I had passed some test that I wasn't even aware of. I smiled. It felt good to be acknowledged. After a few of us had given our interpretations of what consciousness meant to us, Mr. Kwame began to break it down in a way that we could further understand it and use it to gain more positive outcomes. He said, "The way that you choose to show up, is a vital part in the creation of the outcome you wish to see."

He also said that consciousness is the act of being aware of the subtle miracles and blessings that constantly happen daily all around you. As a matter of fact, "the happening" and "it" are one of the same phenomena. As we grow in our consciousness, we fine-tune our mind to pick up on the faster vibratory frequencies that flow through our lives, pushing and pulling us ever so gently towards our dreams and aspirations. Being still and feeling the vibratory energy entering your mind was something he particularly emphasized. "Class, let's take a deep breath in," he would say. We did, and then he said, "exhale with a low audible tone." He then continued to explain that consciousness comes with responsibility; that once you grasp the concept of consciousness and start to become more aware and perceptive of the things around you, you are responsible for the vibe you give and receive. At that point you become blameless - you can no longer say he or she did this, so I did that. You are responsible for your own thought's actions and words...you must take dominion in your life.

He said, "so be careful, my young students; this path is not easy." We all sat there in silence, half scared and half filled with the awkward acknowledgment of our initiation into something important. Mr. Kwame then gave us some homework. "For the rest of the week, I want you to practice feeling and seeing the smaller particles of life. He continued, "what that means is to slow down and notice not only who is talking but how they talk, how their face moves and their body language. I want you to learn to communicate with consciousness." We were all up for the challenge, jumping up like soldiers preparing for battle... little did we know this wasn't that far from the truth....Mr. Kwame smiled and said in a peculiar low tone, "Class dismissed."

9.

"The bike and the pieces that make it go."

One Saturday afternoon, my friends had gathered to go bike riding as they often did on Saturdays (and most days if they could get free time from school and chores). I usually stayed behind on the count of me not having a bike to ride. I'd sometimes ride Big Willie's little sister's pink bike, but I had grown tired of the constant barrage of insults that came with riding a bike with Barbie's face and flowers plastered all over it. So, on days where the crew got together to roll out, I just went to the house to watch my favorite show, *Good Times*. However, on this day, I felt something unusual; as the kids gathered, their laughter, as well as every other sound was magnified to some degree. I was more conscious of it, if you will. I grew restless, and as I stood up and approached the window and looked at the kids zig-zagging in a figure-eight path I began to focus on the different bikes and their parts - I saw the wheels of one and the handlebars of another. I focused on the frame and paint of the bikes as the world began to slow down. I imagined myself riding the bikes, laughing and chasing myself in a circle. I began to feel the joy of riding - I envisioned the warm breeze swishing between my ears, and I felt the pressure of the pedals resisting the force of my feet. My stomach tightened from the trill of almost falling as I leaned too far toward the ground. My eyes closed tighter as the dream materialized in my mind's eye ever more vivid. I took a deep breath and flashes of Willie Sharp's face grinning in approval would appear in my mind. I exhaled simultaneously, spinning on my heels and heading toward the hall that led to the front door. In a trance-like state, I floated out of my house and down the stairs, making a left, taking a few steps and then another left, and heading down the alley into the backyard where my neighbor Carlos, who was the neighborhood bike thief, had established a make-shift bike shop. It was dark and the smell in the air was rancid. But I was only focused on one thing - a bike. It was time to test my new power and take dominion in this moment.

"Carlos!" I shouted. He looked up from his tinkering. I simply looked him in the eyes, staring for a moment and said, "I want a bike." There were no completed bikes around his shop.

only parts scatter here and there He hadn't been out to the white part of town to "collect" any yet, but he saw something in my eyes. that startled him. He asked in a menacing tone, "Man, what the fuck is wrong with you? "I sell bikes, I don't give them away"...I stopped him in mid-sentence with the pointing of my finger; I stood there motionless, Carlos seemingly frozen in time...the supreme eye was in full effect. Then I turned slowly on my heels, like Michael Jackson doing the robot, and walked out. I'd tried out my powers, now I'll wait for the results. I returned to my house, back to the T.V., back to *Good Times*. An hour had passed; the kids were gone to Piedmont Ave. to ride the hills. I sat in my living room on my mother's couch, thinking of the material world - how all things are made up of smaller things and even those smaller things are made up of smaller things yet, and how this continues for eternity. I was so lost in this thought, I didn't even notice the pounding at the door. After a few hard knocks my mother yelled, "Raheem, answer that door boy!" and so I got up and went to the door to see who it was.

Upon opening the door, I saw that it was Carlos.

"What's up Los?" I had almost forgotten my request for a bike just an hour ago.

"Look!" he said, gesturing towards a conglomerate of colorfully painted metal. Only at a second glance did I recognize it as a bicycle of sorts. It had mixed-matched parts, looking more like a hodgepodge of leftover scrap metal rather than something custom made. It had the front wheel forks of a ten-speed attached to the frame of a BMX racing bike. The seat was long, like a pointed yellow clown shoe, the handlebars flared upward and out like the motorcycle that the villain in a 1960's rebel-without-a-cause movie would ride. Each handle was ornamented with tassels that hung at least a foot down; it also had one big wheel in the back and a little wheel in the front for extra goofiness. I loved it, and it was exactly what I needed at the time. It was vaguely what I had conjured up in my mind, although not quite what I had envisioned. That was okay.

I asked Carlos, "Is it mine?"

His reply was short and peculiar. He shrugged and said, "you wanted it, you got it." At that moment I rushed out the door down the stairs and hopped on my bike. I peddled as fast as I could. My feet were slipping off since the grips on both pedals had been worn down to almost nothing, but slipping and wobbling didn't stop me one bit. I headed to where my friends would be; I had to show them my new wheels. On the way I thought to myself that I had to have a name for such an extraordinary machine - it looked bad and tough, as if only a hardcore, vicious dude could handle it. Although it *was* a piece of goofy looking trash jumbled together; for me, it looked badass. I'd overlook the snickers and stares.

Just then, I popped a wheelie for damn near half a block. I decided to call my bike "The Mean Machine." I laughed hysterically. I must have looked like a lunatic sliding around the corner of my north Oakland neighborhood screaming at the top of my lungs, "mean machine mutha fuckah!" I weaved in and out of traffic, the cars screeching to a halt as they tried not to hit me, horns blaring with anger at the little black kid daredevil who seemed to have a death wish. I didn't care about death, getting hurt, or any other consequences as a result of my carefree, fearless self. I was cool, I had freed myself of the pity that other had to bestow on my mentality no one could laugh at me for not having a bike. I needed, I asked, and I received. I was free!

***

It took me some time to catch up with my friends, who were at the top of one of the steepest hills in a small district/city called Piedmont. It was nestled in the back of north Oakland and connected to the Oakland Hills area. We were now faced with the death trap we call "Kill-a-Man" Hill. This hill's real name was 'Monte Vista' and it was the highest hill in the area. Only the bravest of the brave would challenge its formidable terrain.

When I arrived, everyone gazed at my wheels with incredulity; they couldn't understand what they were seeing. Was it a mechanical horse of some kind, brought to life by a wizard? This twisted medley of metal, with its multicolor limbs grasping one another to form a monstrosity of magical marvel. I stood there, letting them bask in my glow of pride. Fat Dave asked in a breathy tone, "where'd u got that raw ass ride from?"

"I had Carlos make it for me. You can't get one unless you're ready to pay in blood."

All the kids gasped at once. Dookie Rob, who had gotten that name by wearing his signature dookie brown tough skin pants, yelled "for real?"

I leaned over with one foot on a pedal, and the other holding me up, saying, "hell yeah, he cut me with a butcher's knife and everything." I was trying to scare them into not wanting one even close to mine. I continued. "I was bleeding all over the place, but it was a magic knife, that's why I ain't got no scars and stuff."

Everybody simultaneously said, "Ohhhhhhh," Dookie Robb adding, "okay that makes sense, cause I was about to say..."

We sat around talking and joking for over 20 minutes, partially because no one wanted to be the first to ride down the path of hellish destruction that awaited us on "Kill-a-Man" Hill. However, we couldn't stall for long due to the fact that the sun was setting, and going down the hill in the dark was utter suicide. One-by-one, my friends dropped into the hands of faith risking a painful demise as they swooshed down the mountain of hill, embracing the thrill of it all. My bravery seemed to deplete, like air escaping from a small hole in a party balloon. Dookie Rob was the last to go before me, and before his descent he turned and looked at me with watery eyes. For a moment I thought he whispered the words, "tell my momma I love her," and just like that he disappeared down the hill, followed by the piercing wail of a child in pure terror. The shrill scream eventually faded into silence, and then was met by cheers of admiration.

It was my turn; however, I hadn't realized that in my attempt to prolong my ride down the slide of torment, I had let the sun beat me on the way down. It was dusk, and nobody had ever attempted to ride the hill in the dark. It was barely just enough to see what I was doing. I crept slowly to the edge, glancing up at the sun, which slowly surrendered to the horizon. I looked down. I could barely see the bottom, but I had to go. *I'm going to die,* I thought. I heard J-Will yelling from the ever-darkening pit, "Hurry up, you trick ass sucka!" and then awful laughter from the rest of the group.

"It's now or never," told myself. I kissed the tip of two fingers and touched the cold steel of the bike, whispering "come on mean-machine, let's ride," followed by "man, forget this! I'm going the other way." I yelled down the hill, "forget ya'll" and started turning my bike around, but as I put my foot on the dull pedal, it slipped off, causing me to stumble over. I was going down the hill either on the bike or on my head; I had to make a choice. I gained my balance just as the mean machine was rolling over the hill.

At first, there was nothing but the sound of wind moving around my body, as if I were cutting through the air and pushing it out of my way like a giant ship pushing through the ocean's surface. I could feel the rumbling of tires as they began to skip over the tar lace street. I left the ground with every slight bounce, my jaws flapping from the air that filled my mouth, and both eyelids peeling back like tiny parachutes trying desperately to slow my fall. But soon, fear gave way to determination. I was like a mad man, yelling and foaming at the mouth, and instead of holding on for dear life I had begun to lean forward to make the mean machine go faster. I felt the front forks of the machine giving way and before I could jam on the breaks, they snapped. Just as I had reached the bottom, they had completely detached from the frame. I watched in slow motion as the forks slid to the right. I slid to the left, head-on into the awaiting traffic. With only one wheel, I held onto the handlebars for dear life, my yelling turned into begging. I zoomed past oncoming cars, missing them by hairs, and finally ran up on the curb zipping between the people walking down Piedmont Avenue. Suddenly, I hit a bump that sent me handlebars first into the front door of a pet shop, crashing into a giant birdcage that hadn't been cleaned in what seemed like a year. Bird feathers as well as the birds themselves flew everywhere. I had lost both shoes from trying to slow myself down, and I felt like I had broken every bone in my body. My elbows and knees were bleeding as the owner, the customers and all of my friends gathered around. I was starting to feel faint when I caught a glimpse of J-Will leaning over me and asking, "can I have your bike?" His voice echoed as I drifted off, then everything went white.

***

I woke up in the hospital with my mother and Aunt Garry sitting on the side of the bed. The doctor was explaining to my mother and aunt that I had only broken my arm, and from the details of the story, it could have been much worse. "Six weeks in a cast," the doctor said. I thought to myself, *that wasn't so bad after all. "kill a man" didn't kill me; I was a superhero!* Well, at least in my mind.

I was taken to a room where my cast would be made and fitted. A short, plump black woman with a big smile entered the room and said, "hello suga, I see you got a little boo-boo." She continued, "well, don't you worry; we're gonna get ya back in fighting shape in no time." She set my arm in place ever so gently and then began to place a strip of cloth under my hand that stretched to my elbow. She then took another material and wrapped my entire arm from my hand to just beneath my armpit. She took a warm, damp rag and patted the wrappings until it started to get warm; the fabric then began to stiffen until it had become brick hard.

I grinned at momma and aunt Garry; they both look amused and concerned at the same time. I had caused a lot of damage to the Pet store; I'd have to make it right. After getting my cast, and momma filling out some paperwork, we were on our way home.

***

Once we arrived home, I asked my mother, "how am I supposed to live with this cast on my arm for six weeks?" Right then, my Aunt Garry laughed and said, "well, your healing process is totally up to you." She said, "did you know that some people can heal broken bones overnight?"

"Really?"

"Sure," she replied. "In fact, I bet you could heal yourself in half the time."

My mother took a deep breath and said, "why don't you ask Willie about the subject of healing someday? Maybe he can give you some understanding."

My aunt nodded in agreement. "That's a great idea."

Later I went off to my room, and my mom and aunt went to the living room to talk as they always did. I got in bed and thought about healing my arm until I fell asleep.

10.

"Every great wizard has a great ally."
- Willie Sharp

The clock seemed to be caught in some ooze that slowed the progression of the second hand. It dragged around the clock's face. I thought to myself, *what time is between time? and how do I escape its clutches?* Tick, tock. Tick, tock. The clock moved ever so slowly. I was relieved when the sweet and glorious sound of the school bell signaling the end of the school day reverberated throughout the halls. Our souls were free from the institute of the doldrums, casting us into sparkling fields of bliss and opportunity.

We all began to move about, packing our belongings into our bags as quickly as we could. Afterward, when we filed out to the front of the school, we all said our goodbyes, signified by lighthearted momma jokes accompanied by soft kicks and shoves. Headed home, I couldn't help but feel today was an unusually normal day. It was melancholy, boring, and uneventful. I paused for a minute, thinking "it's quiet; too quiet." I quickly shook it off.

I had remembered the assignment given to us by Mr. Kwame, and I learned to practice while I had some time to myself. I had realized that stillness was a metaphor and that being still was to come to a reflective place where the smallest particles (observations or details) could be recognized.

You could be still while in motion because, on the particle plane, everything is always in motion. Awareness is the consciousness of the smallest particles. Becoming aware of them will allow you to feel and see them. You'll be able to understand they are the same as you, and are extensions of your body. Therefore, you'll be able to, with practice, control the space around you.

I practiced concentrating on each step I took while walking home. I take a deep breath while taking my first step. I focused on the heel of my foot coming into contact with the ground. Then I focused the weight of my body and shifted it to the center of my foot. I felt the pressure absorbed by my ankle upwards into my shin and calf. It activated my knee, moving upward further to my thigh and hamstring into my hip and spine.

My arms swayed, keeping me balanced on the planet's surface, my neck tilting my head to the rhythm of the concentrated step, and back into position. I exhaled and repeated it again. I did this all the way home, making sure to pay attention, not only to my bodily experience but how the material world would react to the slightest ripple of my rhythm.

After completing my journey to my street, I was jolted out of my meditative state by a familiar voice, one that I had come to have a great deal of disdain for. It was Lamont, a.k.a. Mont "the Merciless." He was the neighborhood bully. His squeaky, almost cat-like voice was like nails on a chalkboard. I cringed with every syllable he spoke.

"Hey, lil ole' stanky, ugly ass boy! You heard me callin' you. Ya must want me to kick you in yo asshole, huh?" He shouted from across 48th street.

I began to walk faster. I was just a few houses away from home. I glanced back and saw that he was starting to come off of his porch. "Hey, bitch!" he said as I broke out into a full sprint. I saw Mont leap from his porch like a lion in pursuit of a helpless gazelle. I finally reached my stairs, but as I tried to run up, I slipped and fell like a helpless white girl in a horror flick. I was dead meat. I thought to myself, *get up you fool*. I leaped to my feet and hopped up the last stair, opened the front door, and slid in the four-inch opening, slamming and locking it behind me just as Mont crashed hard into it, making a loud thud sound. He had some choice words for me from on the other side of the door. I then went to the window, where I saw Mont dancing in the street. He'd stuck his middle fingers up at me, then periodically he'd stop and pace back and forth, mumbling to himself like a maniac. He did this for five minutes before turning and sprinting full speed back to his house. At that moment, I realized two things - 1) Mont was crazy as hell, and 2) that this had to stop. I had to come up with a plan. I couldn't beat him with just pure force; I had to outsmart him. But how? Then, I remembered my walking meditation and how the intention was to affect matter at the purest level and ultimately cause a change in movement of the world around me. I thought if I could convince someone to help me fight Mont, we could then jump him so bad he'd never even think of messing with me again. I pondered long and hard about who should be my subject and co-conspirator on this mission. Just then it dawned on me. J-Will!

J-Will was my best friend. We had met on the very first day that I had moved to 48th from East Oakland. He was a funny-looking dude who wore an afro that oddly resembled the shape of a Christmas tree. I never understood why his hair grew like that, or if it was by choice, but either way I'd always imagine that he was a young magician and his hair was his wizard's hat. J-Will and I were the same in almost every way - the same height, same build, and the same likes and dislikes. The only difference was our ability to breakdance. When it came time to Boogaloo and Breakdance, let's just say J-Will was no "Shabba-Doo." J-Will marched to the beat of his own drum and that beat came from a whole other planet.

There was also one more thing that separated us; J-Will was extremely strategic and methodical. He did things in a way that made adults and kids alike take notice.

The dude was smart, and able to put things in perspective for all people to grasp. He was just the kid for the job. I thought to myself, *if anyone can help me defeat Mont "the Merciless," it would be Jay Mutha Fuckin' Will.* I knew this wouldn't be an easy sale, so I packed a snack bag to help ease my pitch before going. J-Will was very aware of Mont and had his fair share of run-ins with him. Nonetheless, my plan had to be airtight.

Once I had packed the bribe bag with all the special treats like Now and Laters, lemon heads, everlasting jawbreakers, and Icees, I made my way to J-Will's house next door. Since Mont may have been lurking in the front, I used the back door and hopped over the wood-framed wire gate that was covered in long spiraling tendrils of ivy. I crept past the back door of the crazy hot sauce-drinking neighbor, his house set on the same property as J-Will. His name was Ibibio and he was always yelling about something - not the kind of 'upset' yelling but the 'party, celebration' kind. Sometimes he would stand in front of his house and sing at six in the morning. Most of the neighbors had grown used to it and didn't make a big deal about it. As I passed by his back door, I yelled at the top of my lungs "IBIBIO!" And right on cue Ibibio yelled back, "AYYYEE." That was how we greeted each other. I'd yell his name, and he'd yell whatever he felt back. Once I reached J-Will's front door, I knocked and waited for a moment.

I heard footsteps stomping towards the door when I heard a little voice say, "who is it?"

I replied, "it's Raheem."

The door opened and I saw that it was Robin, J-Will's quirky younger brother. He was dressed in a trench coat, Chuck Taylors, swimming trunks, a superman tee shirt, and a black bowtie. This little dude was ahead of his time. I walked through the doorway, which led to the dining room. To the right was a short hallway that led to two rooms. On the right was their mom's room and to the left was their room. Robin walked toward his room and then abruptly stopped to turn around, saying, "I heard what happened on the hill. Did breaking yo arm hurt bad?"

I said, "naw I'm gangsta, don't nothing hurt me."

Robin turned and started walking with a pimp limp and whispered, "yeah, me either."

I walked to J-Will's room and crept up to the door with the intention of scaring him. I snuck up slowly, trying to be as quiet as possible, and then suddenly burst through it, screaming "what ya doing man?" J-Will jumped, startled, looking like his soul had left his body. A couple minutes passed and J-Will came into the living room after having time to catch his breath. Robin and I were doubled over, laughing. I decided to get to the point of why I had come over, but first I opened my bag of treats and

89

threw him a box of Boston baked beans. I waited for him to open the box and take a couple out. I said, "check this out man. We have a problem."

"Problem?"

"Yeah man. You know Mont has been terrorizing this block for a long time. He has chased almost every kid in our neighborhood and I think it's time we do something about it..." I added "before he kills one of us!" for extra theatrics.

"Damn, you might be right; I heard he had stabbed a kid over a game of tag. I heard the kid had tagged Mont and said "you're it" and Mont turned around, pulled out a small knife and said "naw hoe, you it" and poked the kid right in the stomach! The kid started bleeding everywhere but Mont just kept on playing tag running around the bloody kid, singing "you can't get me, you can't get me!"

I just sat there motionless. After hearing *that* story, I was now utterly afraid. But I shook it off; if this was true, it was more imperative than ever to put Mont's reign of terror to an end. I had to get back to convincing J-Will to come up with a plan and then somehow con him into executing said plan. J-Will sat for a few minutes before saying, "the best thing to do is to go right up to his house, knock on the door and when he answers, surprise him with a barrage of punches to the face."

I thought to myself, *that sounds dangerous,* but hey, I wasn't gonna be the one to do the punching so fuck it. I then proceeded to say, "that's a great idea! We'll do it tomorrow; meet me at my house around two and we'll go over to Mont's house together. Deal?" I placed my hand out. Jwill replied "deal" and we shook on it. I headed home.

Later that night I began to think about the next day and what could happen if things didn't go as planned. Like what if somehow Mont was too fast and too powerful to be ambushed, or even worse - what if Mont stabbed one of us? I then thought about Willie. *How could I use my lesson to ensure success tomorrow?* Then I thought that maybe meditation could help, and so I prepared my space, I looked at the time, which read 7:30 p.m., and I took a seat. I began to take deep breaths, counting backward from 10 to 0.

Creating the outcome in my mind, I pictured me and J-Will walking away safely from the altercation. I knew not to try and imagine us hurting Mont, because you can't use the power to harm others. I just repeated the possible happy outcomes of our endeavors in my head, and then I drifted into a deep state of silence. I could feel the air around my head even though there was no breeze. I could feel it caress my neck, shoulders, arms, legs, and feet; the air seemed to flow underneath me. After some time, I could no longer feel the chair that I had been sitting in. Now I was in the creative void, where the grand architect of the universe and I were one, creating the new experiences that would show up on the physical plane. In this place I began to think of love and peace, as well as harmony for all beings everywhere. I thought of the names of my family and friends and I blessed them. I blessed my home, my neighborhood, my city, everything. And there was nothing - no sound, no air, no me. After a moment had passed, I once again became aware of my breathing, which had become very slow and deep. I started to feel my toes and hands as I wiggled them gently. I slowly brought my hands to my face and rubbed my cheeks until I felt present again. I stretched and yawned, feeling content in my efforts.I got up and went over to my bed and climbed in it. I whispered, "thank you," and went off to sleep.

***

The next day I was waiting for J-Will in front of my house; it was 1:30 in the afternoon. I hadn't seen or heard from him, so I wondered if he had chickened out, or even worse, if Mont had gotten wind of our plot and cornered him. Every bad scenario swirled through my mind. *My best friend could be laying in the gutter with a stab wound. At the same time, Mont danced the M.C. hammer around his body.* I pictured Mont's Jheri curl splashing curl activator everywhere while J-Will cried for help. Just then, a knock at the door jolted me from my frightening daydream. I opened the door and to my relief it was J-Will. "What up sucka?" We burst into laughter.

"Come on, it's time to go." It was getting close to wartime. As we made our way across the street we reassured each other with little pep-talks.

As we approached Lamont's house my heart began to pound, and beads of sweat ran down my forehead. Needless to say, I was terrified. When we reached the red-painted steps of Mont's home I raised my foot to signify when we'd begin. I was so nervous I accidentally farted. It was a quick *pop!* Like a cap gun. J-Will shook his head in disgust and said "hey man, let me get in front of you; gon'l kill me before we even get to the damn door!" I was embarrassed but glad he moved up ahead; I didn't plan on fighting anyway.

I whispered, "knock on the door!"

J-Will turned his head and looked me dead in the eyes saying, "Dude, this is yo plan!"

I gulped and reached up to knock, but before I could make contact with the door it swung wide open and at that point, both of us screamed "it's on bitch!" and started to attack. Unfortunately, it wasn't Mont; it was his horrified grandmother standing there, aghast.

"What in the *hell* is going on?" She looked about ready to murder both of us. "And *why* are you on my porch cursing like that?"

I turned to look at J-Will, only to realize he was already hauling his ass full speed back across the street. I looked down to see that he had run clean out of his shoes, then looked up at the old woman, who was waiting for an answer to her question. All I could do was tell her the truth about how Mont had been bullying the kids in the neighborhood and how I had plotted to take revenge on him. After I had finished my reason for being on her porch, she just shook her head and said, "my grandson has a rough life.

"You see," she continued, "when he was a lot younger his father had been shot and killed, and LaMont had witnessed the whole thing. Mont was never the same after, and he began to show odd behavior... he talked to himself. He became very violent toward other kids who he would refer to as 'strange.' We've tried everything we could, but he just seems to be getting worse." She looked off in the distance and sighed deeply. "Last night was the worst; at around 7:30 p.m. we could hear him saying that he was going away. He said, 'everybody would be happy and all the people who he had bothered would never have to deal with him again.'" The grandmother said she thought he was on the phone, but when she went into the room, she found Mont facing the corner, alone and with no phone.

"I was so frightened," she exclaimed, "that I called the police. They came to talk with him, but after a few minutes, the ambulance showed up. They informed me that Mont may have had a mental breakdown of some kind and that with my permission they'd need to take him for evaluation. I gave my consent and they took him away."

I just sat there, listening; part of me was feeling bad for Mont and the other felt relief. As I turned and started back down the stairs, the grandmother whispered, "what goes around, comes around, and ain't nothing free but God."

I stopped and looked back at her. "What time did you say Mont started talking to himself?"

She replied, "right after 7:30. Why?"

I didn't answer; I just walked back home.

11.

"The beginning, I think!

A few months had gone by since I had talked to Willie; meanwhile, my understanding and skill level in practicing consciousness had continued to develop. I was now clear as to what I was supposed to do - I would teach those who sought out the truth in their lives, and on how to achieve their dreams. All my young life, I felt that I had a calling or purpose and that it all had something to do with me, Willie, the old women, and the church.

Today I had gotten up an hour earlier to meditate, as I had grown accustomed to doing for two months now. Clearing my mind before school to remain focused on the universe's relatively transparent materials helped me to stay in the zone of consciousness longer throughout the day. Afterward, I would pick out my clothes for the day, as I had become especially meticulous with my appearance. Now everything had to be clean and pressed; not even a single speck of dust could call my clothes home. I had also cultivated rapport with one of the barbers at Macknificent's Grooming Room, who was known as "Happy Doing' Dan, the mackin man."

Now this brother was *hip*. He knew all the latest hairstyles and all the coldest fashions. Dan and Willie would talk for hours at the shop about dressing to impress, not only for the people who you knew but the ones you had yet to meet. Dan and Willie did all the talking while I soaked up the game, and just like today, I put the concepts into motion. Now that my outfit was constructed I made sure my hair was sharp and neat as possible, with just the right amount of Murray's grease to shine but not turn white like some of the other kids would do when trying to create the wave-like patterns that seemed to cascade from the crown of the head downward, reminiscent of the sun's rays flowing from space down to the earth.

Once my appearance was on point, I made my way to school. When I got there it was 8:00 a.m., and class was starting in thirty minutes, so I had time to hang out with my friends to talk about all the girls who entered and how we would get them to talk to us with our game and wizard-like intellect.

I would give my closest friends tidbits of information so that they could gain access to the same secrets. Some caught on faster than others; however, they were coming along consistently. The school bell rang at 8:30 a.m. on the dot, and we all started to walk toward the doorway of the school building, headed for our classrooms. Through the sea of smiling faces and colorful pageantry of clothing picked out by mothers who wished to hide any suggestion of poverty, I made my way down the hall, exchanging daps, handshakes, and acknowledging nods of approval of those who had followed my instructions on how to dress.

I had finally made it to my classroom, where Ms. Basinger was usually the teacher, only to find out that she had been replaced by a new teacher by the name of Mr. Hobbs. As I entered the classroom, I glanced at his oddly tall and skinny man. He stood like a malnourished tree with icy cold eyes, his face stern and slightly sunken in. I quickly hurried to my desk, but I could feel him following me with his eyes as I walked across the room to my seat. As I sat down, I was met with the words, "Finally."

I quickly lifted my head and scanned the room for the source of the voice; however, everyone was still finding their seats and getting prepared for the day. Then I caught the stare from Mr. Hobbs. He had now gone from a cool smirk to a wide grin in a matter of seconds. Our eyes locked for what seemed to be minutes on end. By this time, J-Will had sat down at his desk to the left of me; he leaned in toward me and said, "Dude, this guy creepy as fuck!"

"Yeah, for real tho."

Mr. Hobbs stood up slowly and stepped from behind his desk to the front of the classroom, stretching his right arm forward. "Silence," he said quietly, his voice hissing like a snake. The classroom immediately became quiet. Mr. Hobbs surveyed the room, looking down his long, pointy nose and continued to speak. "My Name is Mr. Hobbs, and I will be your teacher for the remainder of the school year." He then continued with a strange look of satisfaction, "Ms. Basinger is dead."

All the kids gasped. We were shocked not only at the death of our teacher, but as to the way this news was being delivered to us. Something was not right, and this man's attitude was cold, heartless, and unfeeling. I was afraid. J-Will, so as to not let Mr. Hobbs hear, mouthed, "this mutha fucka is a goddamn *fool.*"

I couldn't respond; I was at a loss for words. I knew this wasn't normal. Once again,

Mr. Hobbs raised his hand and said, "Silence everyone," and again, the room fell silent, save for the repetitive *tick, tock* from the classroom clock that hung over the doorway. Mr. Hobbs continued his introduction. "We have a lot of work to do with very little time to do it, so I will need everyone's cooperation so that my plans will be completed within a suitable time frame."

Mr. Hobbs then returned to his chair, but before sitting down he peered my direction and called out, "Raheem, Ms. Basinger was very fond of you, I am told. I hear you're *quite* the student." He then leaned his head forward, saying, "I hope to teach you lessons you may never forget." A long pause ensued. He abruptly broke his gaze from me to address the whole class. "Class! Take out your math books, and let's get started." A chill had run down my spine; something was going on, and I knew I had to find out.

I made it through the day, but I couldn't shake the eerie feeling that I was being watched. On the way home, I had run into a friend named R.C., and he had mentioned that we had some new kids who came to our school. He asked me if I had met any of them, mentioning how strange they were. I told him that I had not met or even seen the new kids.

"Well, tomorrow at lunchtime, come to the cafeteria, and I'll point them out to you."

I said "cool," and then we walked until we made it to Shattuck. R.C. made a left towards 46th, and I kept straight on 48th down the dead-end street to my house. I looked over at Mont's house, thinking about him and oddly hoping he was okay even after all his bullying. I still hoped he'd get out of the loony house. I got home and greeted my mother with a hug, as if I was back from a long vacation. I asked her if she could call Willie for me. I told her it was important, and that it really couldn't wait. She said to give her a moment and that she'd call after she finished folding the clothes that she had washed earlier. I nodded in agreement and went to my room. After a while, my mother came into my room with the phone attached to the long spiral cord in tow. She handed me the bass of the phone and shoved the receiver towards the side of my head.

"Here, it's Willie."

I grabbed the base with my right hand while taking the receiver with my left, bringing it to my ear. "Hello?"

"Hey man, what's happenin?" came a deep, smooth voice from the receiver. I replied, trying to match the unabridged coolness that Willie exuded. I said, "ain't nothing to it, I just needed to tell you about my new teacher."

Willie was silent for a long moment before saying in a low tone, "okay young blood, let me hear about him."

"How'd you know it was a dude and not a lady?"

"Good grief, I haven't got all winter man! What's up?"

I began to explain my suspicions. "Well for starters, he scares the poop out of me, and I keep getting this strange feeling that he knows me already." I began to break down the ghoul's features, his haunting disposition, how he stared at me, and his weird announcement concerning Ms. Basinger. Willie listened quietly but I could feel his intense focus through the phone. After a while I was beginning to feel like I was right about Mr. Hobbs being more than just a substitute teacher.

Just then, Willie abruptly said, "don't you move a muscle," then hung up. I wondered what in the hell was going on. An hour and a half had passed when there was a loud banging at the front door; it was loud and obnoxious. My mom leaped from the living room couch and scrambled to unlock the door. It was Willie, and he had brought the old woman with him.

12.

"The evils we face.

After Willie and the old woman had arrived, I had an inkling that my whole world was about to change. They quickly rushed me to the living room. Once I was seated, Willie told me to tell the old woman what I had said to him. I repeated my description as the old woman stared deep into my eye. Her eyes glazed over, and I began to focus on her face. The wrinkles she wore were like deep valleys. Her lips were tight and dry. She continued to stare. Once I was finished with the rundown of the new teacher, she leaned back, turned to Willie, and then to my Mother. The latter looked uncomfortable. The old woman proclaimed, "it seems our old friend Hsub has returned."

Just then, Willie jumped to his feet and spun around, one hand on his hip and the other clasped in a tight fist, shooting towards nothing. "Damn it!" He paused, then said, "how did he know about you?"

Curiosity steeped in barely-containable anger dripped off every syllable that came from his mouth. He paced back and forth, darting razor-sharp glances at me. My mother was biting her nails in a nervous attempt to hide her fear. I knew I was in some deep trouble, but I didn't understand what was going on and what would happen to me. The old woman grinned, placed a scrawny, wrinkled hand over mine, and whispered, "be still." In an instant, everything froze. Willie, who had seemed ready to explode, was now calm, his expression motionless. His shoulders dropped immediately, as if he'd been weighed down by sandbags or barbells. My mother took her hands away from her mouth, sitting there peacefully. I felt strangely placid as well, but my curiosity still managed to break through. "So, what happens next?"

The old woman looked at me and said, "well, for starters, we must intensify your training."

"Why?" I asked.

The old woman took a long, deep breath. "Hsub the lord of our enemies has arisen to stop you from becoming a master of the ways of our people." She continued, "Do you remember the story I told you about the RanSan and Nashar people?"

"Yes," I said.

"That wasn't just a story; that is, in fact, the truth of this world."

Mr. Hobbs is not a teacher he is in fact the evil Hsub. He has come to try to destroy our people as he has tried to do for thousands of Millennia. It is your duty to stop him. This is why you must learn and master the skills of the way of our people

I was in shock; this had to be a misunderstanding of some sort. Maybe I had gone crazy, and this was all a figment of my imagination. I just couldn't believe this legend I was told wasn't in fact fiction. A million thoughts ran through my head, and then I heard it - a voice coming from inside my head, but the voice wasn't my own. It was warm and soothing, and seemed to read my mind. *No, my child; this is not your imagination no, not this time.* I remained still, and proceeded to silently ask a question. I said, *Mr. Hobbs is here to kill me, isn't he?* Another voice came out of the depths of my mind and chimed in, saying, *Not if you do exactly what we tell you.* Finally, I heard a third voice, this one the most familiar. *Raheem, please hear what we are saying. You are in grave peril. In order to fight the forces working against you it's imperative that you are equipped with the knowledge and power to do so.* It was the voice of my mother.

The old woman had told me that it was essential to meditate very deeply before sleeping tonight because, in the morning, Willie would be here to pick me up. I nodded in agreement and said, "yes ma'am," and subsequently the old woman and my mother rose up from the couch and headed for the door. Before leaving, Willie paused and turned to my mother. "Make sure he knows before tomorrow."

I looked up at my mother, who looked a bit worried, but a small smile managed to creep up on her face. She looked down and placed her hand on my shoulder, gently guiding me back into the house. As I turned to go in, I glanced over my shoulder to look at Willie, who was helping the old woman into the car. He looked up, catching the direction of my gaze and then winking at me before turning to close the passenger side door.

I plopped down on the couch, my head still spinning from what seemed like an acid trip that happened moments ago. My mother came and sat beside me. She grabbed my hand and said, "baby, I know it's a lot to take in all at once, but you are a special child and it's time you know the truth about where you came from and who you are. You must understand that I never meant to lie to you; I just had to wait until the right time to tell you.

"You come from an ancient bloodline of warrior kings, who throughout their lifetime fought to regain the prominence and status of our people, who were overthrown and cast out of our own lands. Most of our people with each passing generation have forgotten who we were. It is but a handful of our people who are still in tune with our history, customs, and abilities, most of whom you have seen at the first church."

I interrupted my mother. "Are *all* the people at the first church RanSan?"

"No, most of the people are just there to worship because it feels good to them." She continued, "they are just playing along as an alternative to their otherwise normal lives." Her tone became serious. "However, you must be very careful of those people; they can be easily influenced and persuaded to help the Nashar."

There was a long pause in our conversation; my mom looked away at some far off thin; she seemed distant or like there was something deeply troubling her. She closed her eyes and took a deep breath. "Baby, there's something else, too."

At this point I was on the edge of my seat. My mom was being so secretive and cryptic. As if nothing else could surprise me more than finding out I came from a line of skilled, majestic warriors and telepaths!

My mom inhaled once again, her hands shaking. "Willie Sharp is your Father."

Those words echoed around the room, and we both sat in silence for a while. Suddenly I was fueled with a sense of wholeness, and in an instant every inch of the void in my heart and mind was filled with an inexplicable joy. I wasn't just a run-of-the-mill, abandoned kid from Oakland. I was special, and I had a father.

Suddenly I jumped up and yelled at the top of my lungs, "YES, THANK YOU GOD!"

My mom was taken aback at my sudden elation. "So, you're not upset?"

I took a moment to catch myself before shouting back, "*hell* no!" then I clinched both of my hands over my mouth as if to catch my teeth from falling out. Momma looked stern for a moment, before breaking out into a laugh. We hugged and then I bounded off down the hallway to my room. *Man, how could I not be ecstatic at the fact that someone as fly as Willie was my father? Me, of all people!* I felt like the luckiest kid on earth. I went to my closet and pulled out my snazziest pieces, trying to mimic Willie's style of dress. I found a hat that I had purchased a week ago because it reminded me of one the hats Willie had worn. I got dressed and stared at my reflection in the mirror. I resembled him to a t. I couldn't believe I had a father to look up to. I was so excited that I had forgotten about all the other extraordinary events that had happened, as well as the daunting fact that a mythical creature in the form of Mr. Hobbs intended to kill me. I stared and practiced my Willie Sharp impression for about an hour before preparing to meditate.

13.

Preparing for battle.

I lay in my bed, slowly gaining consciousness after a very rejuvenating deep sleep. I figured that sleeping like that was the result of the long-focused meditation session the night before. My attention was jolted to the presence of an intense energy permeating the room. My eyes fluttered and I caught a glimpse of a figure sitting in a chair at the side of my bed, shrouded in darkness. I blinked twice more to gain focus, and I saw that it was Willie. He was dressed in an all-black suit with shoes so polished that they glittered in the moonlight coming through my window. He sported a long, black shearling overcoat that was made of velvet, like the ones from the posters from the sixties and seventies' black love era. To finish off his vicious attack on the uncool, he was adorned with a gold link-style chain that had a medallion, which was encrusted with a large ruby in the shape of the African continent. I sat up, propping myself up with a pillow. I grinned and said, "Dad."

Willie beamed, showing his signature diamond-encrusted gold teeth and replied with the smoothness of a caring pastor consoling a grieving parent, "The great San has blessed me with you, and I must return the blessing by preparing you for the throne, my son." I sat for a minute pondering how I'd convey my next question. Finally I asked "why haven't you come to see me before now?" Pausing for a moment I continued, "why did I have to be without a father for 12 years? The other kids played catch, and were at the baseball games as well as other events with their fathers, but I had no one."

Willie grinned and said replied "Son I have always been here, you were never alone." The fathers of your friends were my brothers. They watched over you and took care of you as if you were their own son. We are a people, who's culture consists of a village. Everyone in this village is family no one is ever left out and neither were you. My brothers stepped in to make sure you didn't go without a male role model until it was time for your training. At that moment I reflected on all the times I went to ballgames and different events with my friends. Willie was right, I was never left out. I smiled.

"I am ready," I proclaimed with enthusiasm. He rose slowly and turned towards the door, looking back at me over his shoulder, and said, "I'll be making some tea for us; get dressed and join me." He continued, "make sure you're dressed to impress; the world will be watching."

I leaped to my feet and dove headfirst into my closet, grabbing and comparing colors and styles. This pair of shoes with that coat, and that pair of slacks with this hat. I thought I was going to murder someone with this outfit! And then it hit me. I remembered that killing someone was a real possibility and that this was a serious matter. My life was indeed in danger and someone actually *was* out to kill me. I sat there in the closet for a minute, consumed with fear. *What exactly did Mr. Hobbs want? What was his purpose for doing these things?* I thought. I also began to wonder who else would be in on his schemes. I took a deep breath and snapped back to the present moment. Maybe the dress code had something to do with my lesson, and ultimately my safety. I began searching for the clothing I'd wear today like I was picking out my armor. I slowed down, focused, and prepared for what was to come.

After gathering my armor, I showered and brushed my teeth. I brushed my hair, making sure not one hair was out of place. I then made my way to the kitchen, where Willie had made a fresh pot of tea. The fresh aroma of florals and mint wafted through the house. I sat at the table, waiting for instructions while I felt the kettle's steam blanket my face.

Willie made his way to the table with tea in hand. He took a long sip from his cup, slurping slowly so as to not burn himself. He inhaled deeply. "Tell me, Raheem, what do you know about faith? And secondly, can you tell me what it is and how it is used in everyday life?"

I sat back. I scrambled frantically to gather my thoughts to deliver a well thought-out response. I wanted to impress Wille and make him proud. I began by nervously stating, "faith...is the practice of will."

Willie paused, his face tense; he seemed surprised at the answer. After eyeing me for a minute a wide grin spread across his face. He then replied, "yes." He continued, "it is the 'Activation of Will' that creates an individual's faith."

"Willpower, right?" I blurted out.

His reply was sharp and direct. "No!" His face softened. "Will… *is* power."

I tried to process what this meant. I thought to myself, faith is the connective substance that magnetizes the ultimate result of your power or "Will." It helps to create whatever your mind can cultivate. I told Willie that I had understood.

He relaxed, slowly reclining back into his seat and crossing his legs. He grabbed a small spoon and stirred his tea, releasing swirly wisps of steam into the air. He tapped the side of the cup twice, paused, then did a third tap for good measure. He used his thumb and three fingers to hold the cup to his lips, allowing his pinky finger to stand alone. I knew lessons were being taught. "Will" was intentions, words, movement, and sounds- all attributes of the intent of your underlining power. Faith is knowing that your Goals shall be met by your Will... Your Power.

This morning's lesson was well received. I sat there grinning like the Cheshire cat, recounting every movement of Willie's display. We finished our tea before I headed for school. My mother was still sleeping quietly in her room. Willie and I stepped out of the house; it was cold by Oakland standards - a brisk 48 degrees. We hurried to the car and got in. Willie turned the ignition and the engine roared to life, music reverberating throughout the car.

On the way there I became nervous, as I understood that this was no ordinary day at school. I dreaded what I would potentially have to face. I was heading into battle - a battle that I wasn't sure I'd survive. I thought about my lesson and how I'd need to muster all the courage I could to deal with what was ahead of me.

When we pulled up to the school J-Will was standing out front waiting. I had forgotten he wanted to show me the strange new kids that came to our school. The car eased to a smooth stop. I dapped Willie with the ancient soul brother handshake, as I had seen the older cats do. I grabbed the door handle, pushing slightly with my shoulder while pulling to open the heavy Cadillac door. Instantly, frigid gusts of cold air hit me as I opened the car door to get out. Then I thought about something - had it ever been this cold in Oakland before?

"What up, J-Will?" I said, quickly abandoning the thought. J-Will quickly responded, "what's up sucka?" His voice rattled in response to the cooler-than-usual temperatures. We both laughed loudly as we scurried into the school's gate and inside the building. Nobody was hanging out on the steps due to the cold.

We had all packed into the hallway on the first floor of the building, waiting for the bell to ring. J-Will intently scoured the crowd in search of the new kids. I noticed my cast started to itch. *Damn*, I thought, *I don't have a hanger to stick down into it.* "I gotta get this thing off soon," I said to J-Will, who turned, and glanced at the cast briefly before returning to his search.

His eyes darted from one side of the hallway to the other. "Raheem, wait until you see these weird-looking cats, you gonna be crackin' up!" Just as he said those words, he froze, staring off into the distance. He clawed at my coat, his eyes fixed on something in particular. Finally, my attention was arrested by the pale olive green face that seemed to float above the rest of the students. The face was accompanied by two others, who shared the same ominous features.

"Damn," I whispered under my breath. I became aware that these weren't just regular kids. The kid in the front seemed to be the leader; he was much taller than the other two by at least a half a foot. All three wore the hair in the 50's style. Their faces sunk in, given the appearance of being older than they were - too old for elementary school. They wore very non-descript, plain clothing that seemed to fade from shirt to pants. They sported grey shoes that reminded me of the old black-and-white gangster films' two-tone colored spats.

As the strangers floated past, the leader and I locked eyes. A chill descended my spine, like ice water had been poured down the back of my shirt. I heard a voice in my head say, *hi Raheem,* and almost instantly I realized who they were and why they were here. The soldiers were now in position, and war was coming.

I grimaced at the leader to let him know I was ready and not the slightest bit afraid. I didn't unlock my gaze until the leader turned away, continuing down the hallway. I follow the trio until they turned the corner at the far end of the hall. At this time, the bell had rung, signaling that first period was about to start. Kids began scrambling to their respective classes. I stood there, fist clenched. J-Will gave me a light nudge. "Dude, what is going on? Bruh, you're staring at those weird-ass kids like you gonna kill them! Are you alright?" I relaxed, unclenched my fist, and merely replied, "yeah," shaking my head to regain clarity. I laughed nervously, trying not to give any hints as to how scared I was, or the danger everyone was in.

I realized I must confront the enemy as fast as I could, but in a manner that was discreet and minimized the most injury to any of the students, especially my friends. I started to class, but I was preparing to do battle. While in my first period, my conscious was again drawn to the threat being in class with my Hobbs, I couldn't help but convey my trepidation. I gripped the edges of the desk my eyes widened, I started to feel a warmness in my feet as it grew to ascend toward my knees and then past my thighs into my stomach area, my chest neck at this point Mr. Hobbs had begun to turn towards me slowly his face began to show worry as the heat reaches its final destination my head. Seemed to be on fire, I could see the wavy lines of steam evaporating from everything in the room except for Mr. Hobbs. Suddenly everything went dark. I was in a black space. I looked at my hands; they were made up of white flames. I then looked down at my body, and it too was pulsating with white light.

I looked up, and to my horror, there stood Mr. Hobbs, ten times the average height. He was covered in a liquid that looked like it was emitting steam. He began to run full speed at me; my heart raced in anticipation of a fight, but at the point of an impact, Mr. Hobbs shouted with a thunderous boom, "NOT YET!"

I was jolted back out of that place to my chair in the classroom. I was covered in sweat; I struggled to catch my breath. I looked at Mr. Hobbs, who had at this time stood up and instructed the class to remain seated. He informed the class that he had to step out into the hallway to catch some fresh air. Before leaving, he walked to the window in the classroom to open it and let the cold air in. The other kids in the class expressed their discontent with the opening of the window in the middle of the coldest day they'd known to date. Mr. Hobb paid no attention to their complaints; he just snarled in my direction and walked off, slamming the door behind him. Several other teachers poked their heads out of their classrooms to inquire about the commotion. The other kids looked confused as to what had just happened, but it was clear to me. This fight wasn't going to be in the physical realm, at least not totally. This fight was a fight that was waged on the mental plane. The bell had rung, and we couldn't wait to get out of the now icy cold classroom. We poured in the hallway, running to other classes and the heater vents that were stationed at the end of each hall. The kids talked back and forth about what they just saw, trying to make sense of it all.

I peered down the hall, past all the other students bustling to their next classes when I saw Mr. Hobbs talking to one of the kids J-Will had pointed out earlier. They turned and looked in my direction two or three times before Mr. Hobbs patted him on the shoulder and then walked away. I was sure this wasn't going to mean anything good for me.

As I struggled to concentrate in the coming periods, I kept feeling as if I'd lost some sense of reality that the world I lived in was nothing more than a faint echo of a dream witnessed long ago. Everything was fuzzy and dull. I made up my mind to immediately report to Willie right after school and to let him know what had happened. The bell rang in my ear, like a howling banshee warning of the danger to come. When it was lunchtime I leaped from my desk, shoved my books into my bag, and rushed to the cafeteria.

It was way too cold outside to hang on the playground and chop it up as we usually did. I scurried down the hall, and just as I turned the corner to head through the double doors I ran smack into the strange kid who had been talking to Mr. Hobbs. I fell backward, slightly losing my balance due to the weight of my backpack. After a few unsteady steps. I regained my equilibrium. There I was, face to face with the enemy. I was locked in a stare down reminiscent of an old western movie; the clock that hung over the double doorway slowly ticking. It was indeed high noon, and the showdown was now on. As we stared, I felt a sense of insecurity in that I had only trained with Willie a few times; was I ready to do battle? I was beginning to feel cold as fear tainted my thoughts. I could feel the familiar sensations creep into my toes and up my ankles. I was being drawn into the other realm and this time I'd have to fight. the fear of the battle was heavy. The thoughts of my unpreparedness clanged on the walls of my conscious mind. I began to panic, almost causing me to resist the energy and weigh me down as it continued to rise. Suddenly everything went completely pitch black, and silence prevailed.

For a moment I thought I had died, but just as I had come to this conclusion I heard an echoing voice proclaim, "you know you can't win here." The sound seemed to slide from one ear to the other, then bouncing off into a million pieces of razor-sharp doubtfulness, eliminating my last remaining hopes of confidence. I struggled to keep control of my mind, but it felt like I had no will to resist. The voice was accompanied by a cold breeze, and a whisper that said, "See, we haven't even begun, and you already lost your faith."

I trembled as the cold air streamed down my neck. I spun around to face the owner of the ominous voice. The little kid that stood in the hallway at school had become a nine-foot tall monstrosity, his eyes boring into mine. His forehead slanted downward into a thick jawline, his nose producing streams of snot that ran down to his thin, dry lips that were slightly parted, revealing a row of four sharp yellow teeth, flanked by fangs. I was frozen with fear; I didn't know what to do.

"You know," the monster whispered. "Willie has lied to you. He told you that you were special; he said you had powers and that you could stop us by using them, correct?"

I could barely speak, but I managed to utter a reply. I said that yes, he did say those things. The monster released a deep, contemptuous laugh. "You fool! You're nothing more than a sacrifice to the great Hsub. He tricks young fools like yourself into believing they can do extraordinary things so he can feed their souls to Hsub as repayment for a debt that Willie owes." I protested that the monster was the one who was lying. He slowly leaned down to make sure my eyes met his and with a deceptive grin he said, "do I detect a hint of hope?"

Before I could answer I felt the mind-erasing blow to the left side of my head, knocking me in the air; it was quickly followed by the sharp impact of a fist to my rib cage on the right side, sending me flying in the opposite direction.

When I landed, I rolled twice before sliding to a stop. I lay there bleeding, covered in bruises and despair. I looked up weakly to see the monster's hand yanking me by my head. He then thrust me into the air and slammed me down onto the floor. I screamed in pain, and again I found myself being hurled into the atmosphere only to collide with the unwavering floor. I began to think of the afterlife. *I'm surely going to die,* I thought. *I cannot beat this monster - it is too much for me.*

Maybe the monster was telling the truth - could Willie have possibly been lying the whole time? Was I just a sacrifice? Just then, the beast kneeled on one knee next to me and said, "ah, yes. Now you understand just how foolish and helpless you really are." He continued, "it doesn't do to believe in fairytales, young boy." His words echoed in my mind. *You shouldn't believe in fairy tales...* I was starting to drift off into the arms of death. Still, the words began to become louder. They started to reassemble in mind, instead saying, "believe, young boy." My brain latched onto these words; I clung to this statement with the little strength I still possessed. I took a long deep breath into my lungs, and suddenly the darkness and pain began to subside. The monster, who had been sure I was going to give up and die and had already started his process to return to reality, stopped when he noticed my movements. "What are you doing, boy?"

I stood up slowly, adjusting my posture as I centered my energy. I exhaled and replied... "Believing." I began to levitate, as if resurrected by the great San himself.

"Impossible; you have nothing and *no one!* You have neither the power nor the discipline to defeat the likes of me."

He began charging at me full speed. I jumped to one knee as the monster had reached full stride, steam leaping from each of his nostrils like a Bull, who had seen the red fez of the ancient Moors. He drew back to strike me with a destructive blow, but I had launched from my kneeling position and initiated a strike of my own, screaming at the top of lungs

At that moment, our fists collided, which resulted in a sonic boom and a flash of light that sent a shockwave, reverberating throughout the dark void. Once the flash of light had diminished, I stood with the monster at my feet, dead. I had believed wholeheartedly that my victory was at hand, and the outcome was manifested through my unrelenting faith. I closed my eyes, took another deep breath, and with the long exhale, I opened my eyes to find myself back in the normal realm, back at school in the same spot I had left, but the strange kid was gone. I had won my first battle.

There was a lesson learned that day, and it was that the forces that govern this world, also have a profound effect on other people; moreover, it was possible to exist in the two realms at the same time. I had my crew of wizards picked, and now it was time to rid the two domains of Hsub and Nashar people forever. It was time to get to work.

14.

Faith and believing in your talents.

The next day I gathered up the troops. There was J-Will, Fat Dave, 'Steel Will' Willie, who had gotten his name because of the steel skates he wore. Then there was Carlos, the bike thief, and Tommy, Wowo, and Erin. The last three were new to the neighborhood, but they had a knack for building things like clubhouses and stick guns, plus they were from Los Angeles. Rumor has it that they were in a gang. In any case, they were from 48th street now. Other members of our team were Dookie Rob and Ibn, two Muslim brothers who lived in the apartments at the dead-end of 48th. Street. We all met in my backyard. It was twelve noon, the sun shining brightly overhead. I had put on a red robe that I had gotten for Christmas. I wanted to channel one of my idols, this super cool dude named Cyrus from the movie *The Warriors*.

The kids were waiting for me in the backyard as I kicked the door open and walked down slowly, to give the appearance of floating.

I started the meeting by saying, "you are all probably wondering why I called you here. Well, let me tell you there is a scourge coming to harm us all! This scourge is a monster who is hell bent on destruction and mayhem, the likes of which you've never seen. SUCKAAS!" I was trying to use a dramatic effect to drive the point home.

My friends just stared at me like I had gone crazy. I continued yelling. "Listen up chumps, this is serious business - ain't no jiving around suckaaaas." There were thirty seconds of complete silence. Then they all burst into uncontrollable laughter. I tried to regain control, but they all just giggled and pointed at me.

Carlos stood up and said, "man, you have lost yo' fool mind," and fell over onto Erin, who was sitting beside him, bent over with tears in his eyes from laughing so hard. I was all out of options, so I got quiet and focused. They needed to understand, but how? I needed to show a display of physical force to convey the truth of all I had seen and learned to my friends.

Just then I got an idea. This was the time to see if I could move the elements of this world, just as Mr. Kwame had taught, so I went inside my mind. I closed my eyes and took a deep breath and imagined the air particles that floated around my face and neck down to my feet. Once

I had felt that I was connected to them, I then started to communicate with the next particle beside the one in front of me, and therefore controlling them. As my field of control grew, I noticed that the wind picked up slightly. My body had dematerialized and mixed in with the particles, but I kept inhaling and exhaling slowly. The wind got stronger. I waited for a moment and took another deep breath, and now the wind howled around the backyard like a tornado. Dirt and debris were flying everywhere; the children were in awe at the display. They all ran to hide and take cover as the wind swirled around me. I looked at them and I took my finger, placing it to my mouth so as to quiet the noise. Just then the wind abruptly stopped. It had worked. I finally had their full attention. Their frightened figures inched closer to me until they were all back in a semicircle. Dookie Rob spoke first; he mumbled, "dude, how did you do that?"

Pointing at my brain with both hands, I replied, "consciousness!" Then I began to tell them the story of Willie and the old women, Hsub, and the Nashar people. I told them that next Sunday, we would all go to the church on the hill to meet Willie so he could explain the rest. Just then, I noticed a shadow flash past by the entrance of my backyard. I knew who it was

- Willie. The reality of what just occurred hit me. I didn't make the wind move; it was Willie all along. He did it to help me gather my crew. I was a little disappointed. However, the fact that it could be done was a comforting thought.

I spoke a little more about the importance of faith and believing in your talents as they developed and manifested them into one's reality. After my speech, all my friends left, and I went into the house to eat. I sat and looked at my cast. I still hadn't learned how to heal faster - I kept letting it slip my mind - but I'd ask on Sunday.

15.

The 48th Street Mob
The Wizards of Shattuck Ave.

Sunday had come, and all the kids were able to make it the church on time for the service. Everyone was anxious to see what the church was all about, as odd and unusual figures milled about the courtyard greeting one another with smiles and hugs. My friends and I stood grouped together like frightened ducklings, scared to venture too far away from their mother. The day was warm, and the slight breeze that drifted through the small crowd agitated the movement of the women's sundresses, giving us glimpses of knees and thighs. It only added to the anticipation of what was to come.

All at once, the crowd began to move towards the sanctuary. We followed. I lead the other boys through the double doors to the long wooden pews, where we sat in the third row from the front. And just as I had suspected, Willie and the old lady were seated in front. I didn't speak, but instead I greeted Willie and the old woman with my mind. *Hello willie, Hello Ma'am.*

They both turned their heads in my direction and nodded. The experience was a bit odd, but I was starting to grow accustomed to the unusual, more fantastical ways of life. Willie looked at the kids and grinned in approval. The sermon went on with the usual pomp and circumstance. Afterward, the boys and I were off to gobble down donuts in the cafeteria across from the sanctuary. Willie found us and said, "so this is the army, huh?"

"Yep!" I said with a big smile. I was proud that I was able to influence my friends to even come this far, even if they weren't quite a hundred percent on board yet.

Willie continued, "gentlemen, my name is Willie Sharp, and I'm just a wizard of the modern age sent to teach you the ways of my people." My friends were entirely enthralled now, leaning into the sentences floating from Willie's face. I knew that look - it was magic, it was the doorway to enlightenment for our young minds… we were about to "step into the future." Willie turned on his heels as he spoke and started to walk. We followed him to an area where chairs had been arranged in a semicircle. Willie waved his hands and one by one, we sat in the seats. There was a long pause as Willie stared at each of us, darting his eyes from face to face seemingly looking for something. "As I expected, all of you here are of kinship. You may have not known this, but it is true. Your souls have rekindled relationships of lives past, and here you all are today, ready once again to take on the task of fighting for our kind. I'm sure by now Raheem has given you the basics on our history, but that is only the tip of the iceberg. What lies beneath the threshold is infinite knowledge, wisdom, and understanding. The journey you are about to take is rife with danger, but if you are brave enough to persevere, then we will be successful."

Just then Mr. Kwame walked up and said, "alright lil brothers, come with me." I had known the lesson that Mr. Kwame was going to give the others, so I stayed behind with Willie. I wanted to get a deeper understanding of my battle with the strange kid, and to also finally ask about the process to heal quickly.

Willie and I walked and chopped it up about the battle. I told him how I had been whisked away to a new place and that the battle had seemed to take hours, even though it only spanned a moment here. He stopped, and sat on a stool that could only have been made for sitting at, while t schooling some young dude on how the world worked; and so there I was once again in the midst of an epiphany but this time I was ready and eager for my latest lesson. Willie leaned back against the tree that the stool was propped up in front of, and pulled out some square sheets of paper, holding them in one hand while he used the other to reach inside his coat pocket and retrieve a pouch. Willie set the pouch on his knee and reached into it, pulling out some weed. As he began to talk he crumbled the herbs in his hand, and I braced myself for the game. "First things first," he said, "what does it mean to heal or to *be* healed?"

I stayed silent. After all, I didn't know the answer, and secondly because I was too busy thinking that he wasn't seriously lighting a joint right here in church! Willie grinned and said "chill little man, the herbs are from nature and we're all about nature; in fact, we are nature."

I still looked around, noticing that no one was even paying attention to the demonstration, so I relaxed. He resumed, saying, "if you want to be able to heal yourself and others, first you have to know that the process by which your body manufactures its health, is all-natural.

"The body has tiny organic robots known as cells, whose only job is to bring oxygen to the damaged area so the collagen can start rebuilding the damaged area. Now, you know about recognizing the particles around you, but what about the particles *in* you? Can you talk with the sub-particles within your body?"

"No, I don't think so," I stuttered, fumbling over my words. "At this point, I know it's possible, I just don't know how to do it."

Willies' face was frozen, and his hands put the final twist on his joint. "You have the key to every door imaginable - and it almost always starts with meditation. Through the proper form of meditation, you can dive deep into yourself and direct the smallest particles that make you, *you*. Just as a bodybuilder lift weights and diets to achieve the final desired result, you too with practice can communicate with the sub-atom particles in your body to do what you expect them to do. Your Aunt Garry always says, 'we grow into our dreams.' Well, a big part of growing into our dreams is the expectation of fulfillment."

Willie paused to see if I had grasped the deeper concept of what was being said. Then he continued, think about it - that's what you do when you have a goal in mind, right?"

"Yeah, I guess."

"Well it's the same process!" Willie exclaimed. "You must go to the smallest things and micromanage them until you reach your ultimate expected goal. This is the journey of growing into your dream. But to heal, there are two parts: first you must reverse the process. Instead of starting small, you will start big with your entire body. You would go into your meditation by taking nine deep breaths, holding them in for nine seconds, and then exhaling very slowly for nine seconds more until all the air is completely out of your lungs. Relaxing your body and acknowledging it are crucial. Then begin with looking at your hands, focusing on the color, then noticing how many scars, cracks, and crevices there are. Notice the pores and try to count them, then focus on the wrinkles as well. Notice the hairs, then become aware that your whole body - your face, your neck, your shoulders, chest, stomach, hips, legs, and feet - all consist of these little features. All skin is made up of tissue. But now here comes the tricky part - the tissue is under the skin, so you have to imagine how it looks until it reveals its true image. Now once you've received the message from your deeper tissue, it's time to go deeper.

"The fat that lines your body covers your muscles, and the muscles are covered with veins that transport the blood cells to every single inch of your body - all this on top of the bones you use to operate your organic machine. Now imagine the material that makes up the bone. Collagen, mixed with calcium phosphate. And these are made up of proteins called proline, glycine, hydroxyproline, and arginine. These proteins are the elements or components you must communicate with. Willie paused, took a long pull of his joint and continued, the smoke drifting atop the words that danced from his mouth. "You commune with these proteins by electrical currents that accompany your thoughts." He raised his voice "words mean nothing to Molecules; your thoughts are the gateway to the light. The electric field! "can you dig it?" He whispered.

I was so overwhelmed from the influx of information, I couldn't speak. Willie grinned; he knew that I was being overloaded with the game, but he continued. "Your thoughts carry emotions, and these emotions make up the vibratory current of information that is transferred to the proteins. The higher the frequency the faster the proteins react, and the lower the frequency the slower they react. The proteins only do their job; whether it be fast or slow. This depends on what emotions, and therefore electrical vibratory frequency, your mind is on."

My mind felt stretched to the max; my eyes felt like they were going to pop out of my skull and lit was very clear - too clear. Willie began to laugh, almost as if he was enjoying my confusion and dumbfounded expression. He then muttered the words "et erit lux" and I blacked out.

I awoke in the sanctuary; I had been placed in front of the altar with all my friends around me. They all looked different - their silhouettes were lined with a warm glow. At that moment I knew they had been introduced to the new world, that they were ready to fight, and that it was time to get busy. I rose from the altar and stretched my hand towards them, and in return, they did the same; in a circle, we made an obligation to the Great San and ourselves - to never reveal who we were to anyone unless they had proven themselves to be one of us, and to protect our people from those who would try and harm us. Last but not least, we pledged to vanquish the Nashar forever.

On the way home, the gang was charged with the energy that came with having a new purpose, or for most of us, our very first purpose. We all walked from the sanctuary to 48th Street; it was only a half-hour walk, even though it seemed worlds away. Broadway terrace wasn't anything like our hood.

We walked and talked about what they had just been told, and Ibn and Dookie Rob were especially quiet.

"Yo, Ibn, you alright?" I asked him. He looked at his little brother and nodded in the affirmative.

"I know it's a lot to take in, but the initial surprise will wear off and you'll be left with complete truth."

Ibn rubbed his chin and said, "I have no doubt in my mind that what I heard was the truth, but that's the thing - it seems to answer every question that I had all my life."

"Well good, brother - I'm glad you feel that way. This is only the surface." I turned to jwill. "You know we gonna have to deal with the rest of those strange kids when we get back to school tomorrow. I'm sure they'll know we've all been enlightened."

J-Will stopped in his tracks. "I'm ready... we are going to fuck they ass *up*!"

We all cheered and gave high fives to one another. We made it to 48th street just as the sun began to set, going our separate ways and promising to see each other in the morning at school.

When momma dropped me off at school the next day, I noticed the crew was already there out at the front. They looked nervous and uneasy. I approached them, trying to show confidence and encourage them. "What's happening gentlemen?" I asked, trying to be cheerful. They didn't answer. "Yo, what's the deal?"

Tommy just pointed and said, "look, man."

To my dismay, there were more strange kids arriving; they had doubled in number. Not only that, but they were also accompanied by older folks, who appeared to be their parents. They stood by their cars, eerily staring at us. *This is going to be a lot harder than I thought,* I realized.

16.

Gang Bangin'
In the Quantum Realm

We all had our marching orders. We all know who we were, and as a group, we now had to take the enemy head-on in every way we possibly could. The 48th Street mob was in full effect. We had to devise a plan. I'd have to think. The bell had rung, and it was time for all the students to go to the first period. Our group exchanged daps and handshakes before reluctantly going separate ways, moving along to our respective classrooms. Carlos, Erin, and Wo Wo all had class together; they were a little older, so their classrooms were located on the other side of the school. Dookie Rob and Ibn had classes in the same part of the school, but both were alone.

At nine in the morning, it was so quiet. Carlos, Wo Wo and Erin sat in the back row of their classroom eyeing the three strange kids who had entered the class. Their teacher tapped her green coffee cup, saying, "class, we have a few new students this morning who have arrived at our school. Please show them a warm Emerson Elementary School welcome." The teacher gestured to the kids as they rose to their feet. The teacher encouraged them to speak. "Go ahead, don't be shy. Tell us a little bit about yourselves."

The smaller of the two spoke first. "My name is One."

Before he could continue, one of the other students yelled out, "'One?' Like the number?"

The whole room erupted in giggles. The strange kids' faces hardened and slowly crept toward the student who had blurted out the taunting question. Carlos stood up, then was followed by Wo Wo and eventually Erin. They positioned themselves between the student and the strange kids. Carlos said "you looking for a fight?"

Their teacher jumped in between the leader of the new kids and said, "now, now there will be none of that please return to your seats."

All parties reluctantly moved back to their seat. Erin and Carlos gave each other a celebratory fist bump. Wo Wo whispered, "shitttt, I was about to knock one's ass out."

The kid whose name was 'One' turned around and said, "you'll have your chance, bitch."

Wo Wo was startled by the response. He thought that no one could've heard him, but somehow, that kid did. For the rest of the period, the two crews continued to eye each other menacingly. The bell disrupted the tension; it was time to see what the strange kids were made of. Carlos led the other two to the door to get in position, but the strange kids were quickly able to slip past, blending in with the other bustling kids who fell out into the hallway, disappearing completely.

"They're gone!" Erin shouted.

"What the hell... how?" Wo Wo exclaimed.

The strange kids had vanished without a trace. Carlos huffed. "Don't worry; we'll find them. And when we do..." his voice trailed off and the three marched on down the hallway.

On the other side of the school, Dookie Rob and Ibn were leaving their classes. It was lunchtime and all the members of the 48th Street Mob were to meet up at the lunchroom to discuss their next plan of attack. Dookie Rob had found Ibn as soon as he could; he was afraid of being cornered by the strange kids alone.

"Big bro!" Dookie Rob shouted out as he ran full speed towards Ibn, not paying attention to the two strange kids who had now managed to get close enough to kick the back of his foot mid-stride. Dookie Rob went flying in the air as Ibn turned to watch his little brother fall face-first toward the ground. Ibn ran to try and help break his fall, but was too far away. His face hit the unwaxed tiles and bounced like a stone skipping off the surface of a pond. He slid across the floor until he came screeching to a halt.

Ibn kneeled alongside his little brother's skinned face. Dookie Rob squirmed in pain, grunting to suppress his desire to scream out in agony.

"Are you alright?" Ibn asked frantically.

"Bruh! Half my face is missing; I am absolutely *not* okay!"

Ibn suddenly leaped to his feet with rage in his eyes. He scanned the crowd, his eye locking dead-center with the kid who had tripped his little brother. Without hesitation, he launched himself like a missile in his direction. Then, there was silence.

Ibn was consumed in darkness, and in his rage he had inadvertently transgressed to the other realm. He could feel his body, but he couldn't see anything. He turned in a complete circle and saw nothing. Then, they appeared as if a curtain had been pulled back to reveal the actors of a puppet show. Ibn, still enraged. balled up his fist and prepared to fight. The kid who had tripped Dookie Rob stepped up and smiled sinisterly. "You've made a grave error, coming unprepared to this realm." He continued, "you haven't been trained in this world, your mind isn't ready, and your friends are just as pathetic and misguided as you are. You are completely alone."

Just then, I cut him off. "But he's *not* alone!" I stood between Ibn and the strange kids, and like a beam from a laser I attacked them with several punches and kicks; one of the others tried to join in on the melee but was deterred by a series of eye gouges and a knee to the stomach, all executed with blinding speed. I laid waste to them. And when the proverbial dust settled, I stood there with the strange kids at my feet.

I looked back at Ibn, who was in total shock at the carnage before him. "Ibn, you good?"

Ibn could only shake his head up and down. I approached him slowly; I knew that Ibn had somehow jumped into this realm by mistake and that could've messed with his mind.

"Try to relax, it's the only way to understand the instructions I'm going to give you."

Ibn took a deep breath and tried to gain his composure. "I'm going to call for help," I told him, patting him on the shoulder.

Out of the darkness, a deep voice bellowed. "You rang?" Then, stepping out of the darkness, was Willie; he walked like a tiger, proud of his cub's first kill. The tone of Willie's voice was reassuring and safe; it felt strong and protective. Willie took a deep breath that seemed to last longer then any human could take, and he released a whoosh of warm air that danced around the dark space. "Ibn," he said gently. "Do you know where you are?"

Ibn quickly answered, his voice full of despair. "No!"

Willie then made a gesture with his hands, waving in a downward motion as to remind Ibn to keep calm. Ibn caught himself and began to regain control of his nerves and emotions.

Tthis is the Other Realm; some would call it the 'real' or 'first' realm. This is where the material of the world you live in is made. This is where the absolute first actions are made; they manifest in the world you know and also in tangible objects and things. We all originally come from this world, but it has been overrun by hsub and his people. Our ancestors once thrived in this world but no more. We exist on the plain that you know as reality. So, this is the place where combat can take place, and you can jump between realms as you please."

Willie paused, then asked, "do you understand Ibn?", to which he replied, "yes."

"Great!" Willie exclaimed, slapping his knees and rising to his feet. "Now, let's get you home to the reality you know. Ibn, you have a gift from the Great San, and you will learn to cultivate it and control it in due time."

Ibn nodding in agreement. Willie started to walk backwards, dissolving back into the darkness from whence he came. A spark of light signaled his departure. Ibn took a deep breath and when he slowly exhaled, he could hear the faint echo of schoolchildren laughing and playing; he opened his eyes - he was back. Ibn turned to look for his little brother, and saw that Dookie Rob was sitting on a bench not too far away from where he had come crashing down to the ground. He walked over to him. "You good?"

"I don't know," Dookie Rob said pitifully. "When you jumped up to fight the strange kids I blacked out, and I could hear fighting and then talking but I couldn't see anything until I opened my eyes, and I found myself sitting here."

I'll have to guild my little brother through this difficult lesson, but for now we need to get to class, Ibn thought.

***

17.

The Meeting of the Mind

Two days had passed without incident. Today, the afternoon sun gave somewhat of a relief from the cold, unforgiving temperatures of the previous days. Willie and I were sitting in his Cadillac. His eyes squinted as he intensely focused on the buttery-smooth rhythm of Parliament's "Motor Booty Affair," which was oozing from the radio. Willie would sometimes say that the whole world existed in a song, but I never understood what exactly that meant. He said it had to do with vibration or something, but in any case, Willie loved his music. But I knew we weren't here to just chill out in the car, enjoying some tunes - we were waiting for a few of his friends. It was time for him and his buddies to have a little sit-down.

Just then, my attention was focused on a stream of colorful cars cascading into the neighborhood like candy-coated roller skates. Sounds blared from the half-cracked windows; playing different funk, jazz, and blues songs that mixed and meshed with one another seamlessly.

These people that had arrived were the Old Wizards, and they had come to gather to pure the gospel of ancient black magic from the days of old into my mind. As each of the cars passed by Willie's, a distinct horn would blow, and I'd see a nod from the drivers as well. Once all had passed and then parked, the street was now filled with cars..

Like a line of choreographed swimmers, they all exited their vehicles. Willie and I did the same. I straightened the long trench coat I had picked out from this morning to match the ice-cold ensemble I knew the brothers would have on. I couldn't help but feel that I should've worn a more colorful shirt that matched my shoes; after all, your style was an expression of your inner state of being. As we gathered in front of the birdcage bar, an old man who I assumed to be the main leader of the group grinned and greeted everyone with fives and handshakes.

"Sappinin' young blood?" A tall dude mumbled, a wide-brimmed hat covering his eyes. I froze, trying to think of a cool response but all I could do was reply politely, "not much sir."

The old man chuckled and continued in a low mumble, "give it time," to which all the others laughed briefly. It was an inside joke, one that apparently only older guys knew. Willie went to the door, motioning for the group to enter. "Shall we gentlemen?" He asked invitingly.

The crew all held their hands in front of themselves, ushering me to go first, so I did. As I crossed the threshold of the entrance, I immediately realized this wasn't the birdcage bar at all; instead it was replaced by a room with neon lights, with the people who I'd seen at the church on the hill. There was a long bar where some beverages were being served by a beautiful woman whom I could've sworn was seven feet tall. Her afro brushed the top of shoulders, framing her soft facial features and full lips. She winked at me while I stared as we made our way to the long table perched in the far corner of the room. Everyone waved and nodded to acknowledge us, and some tipped their glasses in toasting fashion. This was black elegance and cultural pride to the tenth power!

We went to take our seat, Willie making sure to guide me to his left and the head of the table facing the doorway. The waitress came hurrying to the table to take our requests, and one-by-one all the brothers began to order exotic, rare drinks with wild names, from the likes which I'd never heard of.

After the drinks had arrived and some quick small talk and banter, the mood became serious as we prepared to talk about the main reason we were here. Willie tapped his glass of expensive cognac, cleared his throat, and proclaimed, "gentlemen, I've called this meeting at the behest of our distinguished elder and last of the original Council of Usda-Pinea, Shaka RahSan. This is an extremely important and dangerous time we are living in. Therefore, please give him your full and undivided attention."

Willie gestured to the man with the wide-brimmed hat, who slowly set his glass down, pausing for a while and then raising his chin to speak. "Brothers, since the days of the exile of Hsub, we have been in danger of annihilation. Our people have been chased to all the four corners of two different realms, and still, we run and hide waiting for the day to regroup and finally strike back, ridding the realms of Hsub and the Nashar people forever. It has been brought to my attention that the missing key has been born and that the vibratory frequency has been reached."

Shaka looked down the table at me and pointed. He exclaimed, "the key is with us, and we must give him and his army the necessary tools to fight." Everybody in the room was silent, some nodding in agreement, others whispering among themselves. Willie himself seemed to be consumed by emotion as the elder spoke of retribution and conquest. Shaka began to speak of the old ways and how we as a people lived in harmony with the materials of existence; how the Great San blessed us every single waking moment. Once again, he leaned forward and stared at me with concrete focus as he explained the answer to a question that I had only just formed in my mind. He answered, "yes! the Great San is the cause of all. And so, you wonder why he doesn't just rid us of Hsub? Well, because we as a whole have forgotten that the Great San lives through us! It isn't the great San that must move; it is *we* who must remember to strike on behalf of him, because we are his living and breathing representatives in all of existence."

Just then it dawned on me - that these people have been concentrating on survival for so long that they had forgotten who and what they are and how to protect themselves from the evil that sought to consume them.

I felt a warmness emerge in the pit of my stomach; I leaned back to give it room to grow and that it did. Out of nowhere, a high-pitched ring came out of nowhere and then light began to emit through my clothing; I looked around to see us all in the same state, glowing until the light filled the entire room. In that moment, we displayed a unity and strength that could withstand even the most formidable of foes.

And just like that, I was back sitting in Willie's car, with him listening to his funk music, as if nothing had ever happened. The line of flashy cars dissipated as they each pulled away, driving off in different directions. The meeting of the council was over, but there was much work to be done. I reached for the door handle just as Willie reminded me of the task. "Remember, son; you are the key, and you and your young friends must save us all."

I looked up at him, for the first time fully understanding the weight of the moment. "Yep." I then opened the Cadillac door and exited the car, closing the door gently behind me. I walked towards my house in deep thought. *How could I go from being chased by the "shittaz" to now being the key to freeing my people?* I quickly snapped out of it, because I knew I had a quest ahead of me and couldn't afford to dilly-dally in limiting thoughts. I had to round up the gang and devise a plan.

First, I called up Carlos and told him that we needed transportation. We needed him to build the fastest bikes ever made. I called Tommy, Erin, and Wo Wo as well, explaining that we needed a fortress or hideout - some sort of safe space that could withstand an attack or at least hold off an enemy. I also called Ibn and Dookie Robb, who were especially gifted in traveling to and from the realms; this skill would make them a perfect pair of spies. Finally, I told J-Will that he would be our strategist; he'd come up with our plan of attack and organize our moves. He agreed and said he'd ask his Dad, Mr. Williamson, to help him. He was a Vietnam vet who saw a lot of combat. I surveyed my plan, satisfied that the stage was set - all the players were in place, we just needed guidance from the council and *boom!* It was on.

Early the next day I got a call from Willie. He told me to assemble the squad in my backyard and that he and Shaka would be there to facilitate the lesson. He said that we all need to be prepared to receive a lot of information. Another member of the council, "Crazy J" Mitchell, would be joining us; he was a fierce warrior who had fought in the old days; it is said that he once vanquished ten Nashar with just a stick and twelve inches of yarn. He was a legend and he was coming to help us win - but how he was still alive after all this time, I could never know.

I called the group and had everyone meet me in my backyard at noon sharp. The sun beamed down, its rays brushing my back, almost as if to reassure me. While we waited patiently for the elders to arrive, we discussed the mission at hand. Carlos spoke first. "Hey ya'll, I haven't been able to sleep ever since the meeting at the first church."

The rest of the squad muttered in agreement. Wo Wo even added that when he did finally fall asleep, he'd have vivid dreams and nightmares. Just then, a hardy laughed bellowed from the alleyway that led to the yard, followed by a high pitched but raspy voice.

"That's a good thing; do not be discouraged lil man. It is simply your mind recalibrating to be able to drift between realms. It is a sign you are developing."

We all stared into the alley as Shaka, Willie, and then Crazy J materialized out of thin air. We all greeted the three-council member with excitement.

Crazy J yelled abruptly, "form two lines, one on the north side and the other on the south side of the yard."

We quickly rushed to fulfill his request. He then ordered us to face directly in front of one another; this we did immediately. J then walked up to me and said, "I'm going to tell you a particular word, and this word you must tell the person directly in front of you."

This seemed no big deal to me, because I had already learned the telepathic ways of communication from Willie. I grinned at Erin, who was in front of me across the yard. J leaned in to whisper in my ear, cupping his hand around his mouth to avoid Erin reading his lips. He whispered slowly, "tajmid."

I was prepared to send the word to Erin but was unable to do so; my mind seemed to be stuck in a loop. I heard the word over and over again until I could only focus on it. Then, that familiar light grew from the center of my vision and I instantly knew I was going to be transported to the other realm. I expected to see the same familiar darkness; however, when I arrived, I only saw that my squad and I were surrounded by snow and ice. We shivered from the blistering cold that lashed out on our exposed arms and faces, inflicting painful welts. The chattering of our teeth sounded like individual dice games happening all at once. Crazy J appeared in a full, luxurious mink coat, and it took everything in me to not narrow my eyes at him as he proceeded to whip out a steaming mug of hot tea, the steam disappearing with the chilling gusts of wind that swirled past. His demeanor screamed attention.

We all tried our best to stand as erect as possible, but the cold caused us to double over and it folded our frames like origami. Crazy J grinned diabolically as he once again barked out orders. "Stand up, you worms! This what you're up against and if you can't battle a few drops in the temperature, how do you expect to save your own people from certain death? Straighten up!"

He rushed over to Ibn and got right in his face. "So you're the one who can naturally move between realms without any training, huh?"

Ibn, although freezing from the bitter cold, replied confidently,"Yes sir!"

Crazy J leaned back and said, "show me."

But before Ibn could demonstrate his talent, Crazy J held up his hand to stop him, saying, "wait! Going in and out of the two realms is too easy for someone like you; I instead want you to show me how you can exist in *both* realms at the same time." He continued, "if you can do this, you and your squad can leave here, but if you can't, then you and the rest of your crew will have to stay here and find a way to survive for twenty-four hours. Deal?" Ibn agreed through his jittering teeth.

Ibn managed to take a deep breath of sharp air, exhaling it. He noticed that the air was warm when it left his body, and that gave him a comforting yet brief respite from the howling words around him. He immediately took a deeper breath, holding it, and trying to conceive in his mind an image of home. He released the warm air from his lungs and relaxed. In the present moment he felt a slight warm, fuzzy feeling on the inside of his chest. He closed his eyes again to envision the fire of the sun. He could almost feel the heat of the flames that licked and danced from its surface.

Ibn opened his eyes to see that the squad was back in the yard, but everyone was still shivering. Ibn quickly realized that this was an illusion orchestrated by Crazy J. Ibn smiled, satisfied with his assessment of the situation.. Then suddenly, *Snap!* Darkness cloaked his surroundings.

There was no cold, no warmth, no nothing. Dead silence prevailed. What seemed like hours had passed in the darkness, but it eventually became comfortable and serene. A bell tolled in the distance, making a faint *ding, ding!* My consciousness was drawn back to the moment. I gently opened my eyes to see that we were back in my yard. Ibn had passed the test. We were still in our rows seated towards each other. Willie and the other two council members were standing to our right, side-by-side with Shaka in the middle. Shaka spoke calmly. "The ability to place your mind in a place different from your physical body is very important in this time; you must be able to concentrate on the mission while your flesh is undergoing great stress. Only under extreme conditions can you remember from whence your power comes from, and withstand the circumstances of the moment to achieve your goal. Brother Ibn has shown you the way, and now you must learn for yourselves through his instruction. You all possess the ability to rise above or resist the pain - the Great San and the Ancient Council has deemed it so."

And just as they had come, they exited through the alleyway, disappearing into the darkness. Once the council members had gone, we surrounded Ibn and congratulated him with pats on the back, daps, and cheers. I noticed there was something different about him; he seemed more mature. There was a new look about his face, that suggested confidence in his newfound abilities. I'd be sure to ask him about it, but for now we relished in the moment of good times.

Later that day I was able to talk with Ibn, as I wanted to see if he was holding some information. When I got the chance I yelled, "yo Ibn," looking around to see if anyone was around who would invade on my private inquiry.

"What's up bro?" he sheepishly said, half knowing what I was about to ask. I paused for a second, not sure if I should proceed in my interrogation, but curiosity got the best of me. "I can see that there's more to be discussed, so what's the deal buddy?"

There was a long silence. Ibn stared off into space, as if he was searching for the right way to answer. "Dude, while I was suspended in between the two realms I was able to see the future and past, and in that future, I saw death."

"Death?" a chill ran down my spine.

Ibn hesitated, not sure if he should continue. "I saw *your* death, Raheem."

I froze. How could this be? Shaka proclaimed me as the key; The key can't die! "You must be mistaken!" I hoped he was joking.

Ibn took a long, deep breath. "Naw man, it was as real as real could ever be." He continued, "If you go into battle, you will die." This statement made me sick to my stomach. I got up to walk away, my mind hyper focused on certain doom. I needed to call Willie to truly know if this was real, because the fact of the matter is, I was scared.

Once I got to the front steps I realized I had to tell my mother what I had just heard from Ibn. I started up the steps, each one feeling steeper and harder to climb than the last. Before reaching the top, I opened the door and to my surprise, there was Willie and the old woman. I instantly broke down in tears and explained to them what Ibn had told me. I ran to the old woman and hugged her. My mother and willie looked on with obvious concern etched in their faces. I was then ushered into the living room and onto the couch where my mother and Willie followed.

Willie spoke first. He turned to the old woman, saying, "Mother, can you explain this to your grandson?"

She nodded in agreement, then lifted my chin with her small, shriveled hand to look me in my eyes. "You are not who you are; you are who you'll *become*!"

I was beginning to sit up straight, trying to understand the statement. I was struggling. I wiped my eyes between each sniffle of snot that I tried to save from dripping down onto the old woman's dress. I was confused and she knew it. She looked at Willie and my mother; they collectively took a deep breath and like always, the tension I felt was released. Then she began to elucidate her riddle. "In all of the great holy books, there are characters who are given a challenge or a quest, in which they must fulfill some specific goal or retrieve an artifact that will unchain the minds and bodies of their people. In all those books the people who complete their mission receive a new name, a new self-ideology, and ultimately a new physical appearance."

Suddenly a light bulb went off in my head. "We grow into our dreams," I blurted out. The old woman grinned and replied, "yes, as your aunt Garry says, 'you grow into your dreams', but deeper still is that the mission you accept holds the key to your growth - it is the hardships and trials that you must undergo to reach the end of your quest. Those are the things that will truly refine and mold you. At each level, the person that you think you are dies until there is nothing left but the real you. See, Raheem, we all die, only to live again as a new self, a higher self for eternity."

I fell back onto the cushion of the couch, realizing the weight of what I was just told. I tried to grasp the understanding that I, right here and right now, was a vessel through which the great San would exist temporarily, in order to fulfill his work through a designated person. The great San is constantly evolving, learning through us as experiences. The enemies were just trials to which we collectively used (and defeated) to return to our true selves. They come to us to remind us of our path. Death was not the end; it was the ultimate doorway to infinite life. *What a relief,* I thought to myself. I couldn't wait to tell Ibn that he was right and wrong at the same time.

I also realized that the exercise that Crazy J had put us through wasn't just about his new ability to exist in the two realms, but also about the lesson I just received. Willie suddenly spoke, breaking my train of thought. He said, "As you can see, you must always be prepared to receive a lot of information - nothing is simple, but complex and layered like a sandwich, nuanced and riddled with different avenues and possibilities." He continued, "you eat don't just the bread, or just the cheese, and so on and so forth. You eat the whole thing, digesting each layer, each doing its own thing and making its own contribution to the whole. It coexists together with the other components or ingredients and works together to supply the body with what its needs. That is why you must always keep your eyes and ears open for the signs and information, and be willing to examine and appreciate them from every angle."

"I understand," I said, nodding my head. I felt a sense of calm wash over me. I got up and said my goodbyes to the old woman and Willie. I had grown tired from all the excitement and I needed to take a break from it all and let my mind relax. I went to my room and sat for a long while. Time was inching closer to the war. It was all I could think about.

"And now we find ourselves closer to the day of reckoning," exclaimed Crazy J. It was yet another day of training and we were once again in my backyard, listening to lectures and going through exercises to strengthen our minds and bodies. There had been a physical fitness portion of the routine that had been implemented and although I hated it, I began to understand it more with each passing week. We all seemed to transform and grow in our own unique ways, honing specific capabilities special to us. Our intellect became more astute as well.

Willie also gave us clear and stern instruction that while at school, we were to avoid any confrontations with the strange kids and Mr. Hobbs. Of course we agreed - the less encounters we had with them, the better. We ignored the jeers and taunts from the enemies to further our growth. This was war, and nobody goes into war unprepared. We had to make sure we were doing all we could to put us in the best position to fight our enemy.

The school was letting out soon, June was coming and with that came the summer heat. Crazy J, Willie, and all the members of the ancient council agreed that summer was the best time to strike because it was the time that our people were at their strongest and the Nashar people were at their weakest.

Tommy, Erin, and Wo Wo had built a clubhouse in the back field behind my house, just beyond the backyard. This field had been empty for as long as I could remember - it's where we would play football and dig for salamanders. The clubhouse was a palace in my mind; it had a large main room, and a flight of stairs that led to a small balcony which was equipped with telescopes to see the enemies coming from far off. Whoever funded this endeavor - I couldn't tell you.

We had furnished the clubhouse with an old office table and its chairs; there we would hold our 'meetings' sitting around the table like a junior council. I would relate the wishes of Shaka and the real council to them there because, at this point, I was the only one of us who could go to the bar and sit with the old wizards.

Carlos had managed to build a small fleet of bikes; they were the fastest bikes in the city, at least according to my standards. We began cruising the neighborhood on patrol, keeping an eye on the Nashar, who had unfortunately flooded into the Shattuck area. We would make mental notes of their whereabouts and report to Willie. Sometimes we would post up at the corner of the boy's club, watching the action.

One day we were hanging out when Carlos noticed one of the Nashar soliciting one of the neighborhood workers, an O.G. named Queen Ester, as she stood on the opposite corner of our crew. Carlos gave me a mild elbow and whispered out of the corner of his mouth, "Hey man, ain't that one of the people?"

I looked in the direction he was referring to. "Sho' is, blood."

Fat Dave turned his back to the scene, facing us. " But hey man, shouldn't we press this sucka?

"Naw brotha, Willie said no action til the proper moment. Ya dig?"

169

Fat Dave looked off to the left as if he was contemplating mutiny. He had been pretty much left out of the serious dealings since he went to another school; even though he was from 48th he wasn't allowed to hang out with the neighborhood kids a whole lot - he went on the bike rides and stuff but that was mostly it. I think his parents didn't approve of my friends' ways of doing things. But Fat Dave still hung out with us when he got the chance and none of us seemed to care. We treated him as one of our own. He was just a cool dude with strange parents, and that is what we all thought. We just observed the surrounding scene for a while, until I came up with an idea. I told Dookie Robb to make it a point to ask Queen Ester about certain clients of hers and how often they would visit. Dookie agreed to the task and the plan was in motion. By this time the sun was setting, and a brand-new school week was upon us, so we eased down 48th street dead-end to our houses for the evening. Tomorrow we regrouped at school.

Monday, March 29th was first period at the schoolhouse, and J-Will and I sat in the back of the class, where we had moved to be as far as possible from Mr. Hobbs and the strange kids. Something about today made it hard to avoid the mean looks and peculiar gestures; it's as if Hobb and the strange kids were planning something. I told J-Will to be on guard. "I think something is going to happen today," and almost simultaneously one of the strange kids slowly rose to her feet and turned towards us, her eyes narrowing.

"Aww man," J-Will groaned.

"It's on," I whispered back. She started towards us in a slow, haunting manner, as if she were some sort of corpse or zombie. She floated closer, her feet seeming to barely touch the ground. I took a deep breath and in a flash, I was catapulted to the other realm. Darkness surrounded me; I was met with silence until a faint giggle broke the plain of my consciousness. I remained calm, the footsteps growing closer and louder, closer and louder, until a vision was to be made out in the expansive abyss. It was the girl - her pale face glowed against the black backdrop, but not with a warm, inviting light - it was more of a dull, sickly, eerie glow. Her face twisted into a half frown, half sinister grin. "Where's your friend?" she asked tauntingly. "Is he not brave enough to come to the real world?"

By now I had realized that up until now J-Will hadn't leaped here. Her laughter exploded. "It doesn't matter; i'll destroy you one by one. It isn't as fun all as wiping you all out at once, but this will do."

I prepared for battle, a long standoff between me and the strange girl took place, like two grandmasters of chess calculating their best strategy. We circled each other and just stared for quite some time. The intensity grew to an atomic pressure that I felt in every molecule of my body. I had to strike first, but as soon as I attempted to move a sonic boom accompanied with a lighting flash blinded me. I covered my face so as to block the blow I was sure to receive, but to my surprise, it didn't hit me. I heard a scream, and I removed my arms to regain my field of vision, only to see the girl flying backward into the distance. J-Will!

He walked up to her and delivered yet another crushing blow to her stomach, followed by a roundhouse kick to the side of her temple. The girl fell to her back and slid a few feet or so. The silence was restored. J-Will looked back at me and gave ME the thumbs-up signal; I nodded in approval.

At that very moment, the girl's eyes popped open and she rose like a resurrected vampire, waking from a day's sleep. The look on my face alerted J-Will to the situation, but it was too late - the girl had leaped to her feet and launched herself directly into his chest at incredible speed, like a 300-pound lineman from the national football league. They both went flying, but with J-Will being on the receiving end.

Her back was turned towards me, so this was the perfect time to strike, but when I moved into position I felt a hand clasp my shoulder, spinning me around quickly before I knew what was happening I was met with a vicious blow to the face. I felt blinding pain and then weightlessness as I was lifted off my feet, only to land awkwardly on my shoulder and neck. Another strange kid had arrived at the battle as a reinforcement.

I regained my focus and got to my feet, looking over at J-Will and the girl, still engaged in combat and exchanging strikes and kicks. The girl had managed to scratch J-Will across his face, which was now dripping with blood. Meanwhile, the other kid let out a battle cry and came full speed at me, and I settled into position waiting to counterattack, as Crazy J had taught me. Once the kid reached striking distance he threw a super-fast punch, to which I caught with the side of my forearm and then hooked his wrist with my curved hand, simultaneously using his force to guide him in an upward motion. I then slammed him into the ground, and immediately I jumped down on his back and began a flurry of strikes to the back of his head. After some time, there was no movement from his lifeless body. I stood up to see J-Will viciously ripping the girl's arm from her body and using it to slap her in the face. I just looked at him kind of disturbed and said, "Geez man, was that necessary?"

He just raised an eyebrow, pointing down to what was left of my opponent's unrecognizable head. "Looks like it wasn't enough!" We both burst out in laughter.

In a flash, we were back in the classroom, the two strange kids nowhere to be found. Mr. Hobbs was there, breathing fast and deep. He was furious, and I felt that J-Will and I had just disturbed an ancient, malicious beast.

The bell rang and J-Will and I rushed to the door only to be blocked by Hobbs. He looked down at us with bloodshot eyes, saliva seeping out the corners of his razor-thin lips. He spoke through clenched teeth. "This isn't over - we are coming for all of you and I promise, you *and* the council will all be annihilated!"

We both darted past him, and we ran until we reached a place where we felt it was safe and out of sight. I told J-Will that I was leaving school; I had to tell Willie that war was imminent. I told J-Will that I'd be back, but he insisted on going with me. "Hey dude, we gotta tell the others what's happening as well. It isn't safe for them, either."

I nodded my head in agreement and we set off to warn them. We went by all the classrooms where the squad members were and informed them of what had taken place and that we were leaving. To my surprise, they all agreed that they would accompany us to the birdcage.

As we approached the bar, the usual sounds escaped from the slight gap in the front door - *"I went downtown about a month ago, to see my momma and ma poppa and all of the folks -"* the song's lyrics bounced over a funky groove orchestrated by the James Brown Band. We all instantly felt relaxed, cool, and more importantly, safe. I told the boys to wait outside while I talked to the bouncer. I then turned Super Willy and said, "say, we got some heavy stuff poppin off and I need to speak to Willie ASAP. Ya dig?"

Super Willy just grinned and said "I know, we've been waiting on you," he said with a deep, bellowing chuckle that sounded more like a truck having a hard time starting up than laughter. I shook my head, spun around on my heels and started in. But before I could open the door, Super Willy shouted, "hold on little brother, aren't you forgetting ya peoples?" I was thrown off because up until this point I was the only one of my peers who was allowed in the birdcage. I looked over at my friends, who I knew were anxious to enter this prestigious club, so I gestured to them to come on in. I turned, opened the door, and led the way.

Once inside I noticed that the club inside had yet again changed. It was no longer a place of leisure or excess; it had been converted into a command center of some sort. There were screens showing surveillance of nearly every street in Oakland, and personnel with headsets sat on the consoles relaying information to one another in rapid succession. As we were ushered towards the back room, a young woman dressed in a suit approached us and passed out water to the group. She gave us a slight briefing while we entered the meeting already underway. We all took seats in the back of the club where the council members were seated. Crazy J was speaking in front of a large screen, which had black and white dots covering certain parts of the city. As I listened, I realized that the black dots represented our people and the white dots represented the Nashar. I could see the Nasher had positioned themselves around the Short Shattuck, Bushrod, and Gaskill neighborhoods in North Oakland. These were important sites because these locations were where the San had migrated to throughout the many centuries. The Nashar people were not just in Oakland, either; they had infiltrated all areas of this world and had managed to become part of its infrastructure and politics. This all coincided with the scheme to wipe out the San people.

"The San had been hunted and oppressed for a long time, but this ends now," Crazy J said with strong conviction. "We are going on the offensive. Raheem and his crew will lead the charge. Mumblings of concern immediately rumbled through the medium-sized war room. "Silence!" shouted Shaka. "Have you forgotten the prophecy? Do you not know the way of the San? It's written that the one to save our people from this vibratory destitution we now live in, is the one of the shea'arp lineages. Do we not agree that these young men are the true descendants of that great warrior sector of our people? If you have doubts, let it be known now. Stand up and express your qualms!"

The room was as quiet as the surface of the moon. Everyone looked around for a San brave enough to tell Shaka he might be wrong. After a brief moment, Willie stepped out of the dark corner where he had been observing the conversation. "Until I received word from my mother, I'd truly believed that Crazy J and I were the last of the warriors. But, I have studied this kid from day one. Unannounced to him or his mother, I had followed these boys every step of the way, most especially Raheem. I was there when he took his first steps, and when he learned to talk on his first day of school. Behind the scenes, I gave him the ideas and sparks of wisdom that guided him home to us. I always knew who he was - my son, a warrior, and a wizard. A true Sansman!

"His teaching started years ago and as for the rest of his squad, I was there too, in the disguise of a coach, imam, or a desire that helped to cultivate talents which encouraged them to build with their hands, and innovate. You are now witnessing the rebirth of the natural might of the true warrior class of San, so I ask all of you -" he gestured towards all the people in the room - "ARE YOU READY TO FIGHT? ARE YOU READY FOR FREEDOM?, ARE YOU READY TO DESTROY YOUR ENEMIES AND RESTORE PEACE TO THIS GOOD EARTH?"

Everyone responded with a cheer of confidence. Willie paused and stared at us for a while, then with the hush of the crowd he shouted, "we shall be the victors!"

The place again erupted into cheers and screams of jubilation. We all joined in on the celebration with a new sense of importance, but in the back of my mind I was extremely afraid and as I looked at the others, I could tell they were afraid as well.

The others all got to work with planning our strategies, but the first thing is that we had to was find out where the main hub for the Nashar was. The Nashar weren't like the rest of us; they could only come to this realm through a mechanical device that opened a pathway for them to stay here in the physical state. I remembered that I had Fat Dave, and that Queen Esther was our inside person recording the intel on the Nashar's tricks and whereabouts. I sent Ibn to see if Fat Dave had gotten out of school yet and to see if he had gathered any info from Esther. We needed that info as soon as possible. Ibn agreed and headed out to his house. While he was gone I resumed planning for the attack.

Ibn made his way down 48th Street from Telegraph onto Shattuck. He focused on the car that passed by - he knew that the Nashar were looking to hurt any San they came across, and he increasingly noticed sideways glances he'd get from drivers. He walked quickly down the street closer to Fat Dave; he was getting nervous and could feel the tension in the air, like he was being watched from all directions.

He breathed a sigh of relief once he reached Dave's front steps. There he rested for a second, trying to calm his nerves a bit before going to talk with him. Almost instantly he was disrupted by the screeching of tires and before he could turn to see what was happening, he was quickly covered by a dark hood and punched viciously in the stomach, air exploding from his lungs, unable to scream. He was then met with a second blow to the head, a jolt of pain, and a tiny flash of light. Silence then engulfed him.

Ibn slowly regained consciousness, his head still throbbing from the surprise attack he had endured. He realized his ankle and hands were tied together, and that he was sitting on a block of pure ice. The air was thin and cold, and his shoes and socks had been removed probably so that his feet would have to bear the feel of the icy snow. He let a groan of agony escape his frosty lips, which were turning blue from lack of circulation. He could hear the crunch of the snow under the pressure of someone's feet as they crept closer to him.

Once close enough, the dark hood was removed to reveal a a bright, blank wall. It was so bright it burned Ibn's eyes, and he had to squint to get a glimpse of his captors. Looking up to see the face of his enemy, he was frozen in total shock to see that it was none other than Fat Dave's dad, accompanied by Fat Dave himself!

"What in the world?" Ibn shouted in complete disbelief.

Big Dave just laughed and said, "surprised, are you?" He continued ,"did you really think that you weren't being watched by us, as we were being watched *you*?"

Ibn gulped.

"Your people are fools! We have the whole city surrounded; your people could not have run forever. General Hsub was always confident that he would find you all and here in this city, we have you cornered. Now we shall obliterate all of you, starting with you first."

Fat Dave slowly rose to his feet and walked closer, while making an odd gesture with his hand as if cultivating a round ball. Instead, a slender piece of ice began to grow, hovering between his palms. It ultimately took the form of a sharp knife. Fat Dave paused and the knife glided towards his right hand. Gripping it, he inched closer to Ibn until he was face-to-face with him. Fat Dave slowly bent down to Ibn's left ear and whispered to him, and then standing quickly with a menacing look of pure evil he raised the knife as high as his arm could reach, and with an angry scream he brought down the icy knife directly into Ibn's chest. Ibn could only think about Dookie Rob as he grew more and more cold, his eyelids growing heavy and everything fading to black.

Back at the birdcage, the scene was frantic; all of us were in some sort of group preparing different strategies of attack. Going over different scenarios for a different area, we noticed all at once that the information needed to complete our plans hadn't arrived yet. *Where was Ibn? Why hadn't he returned from Fat Dave's house with the whereabouts of the Nashar's portal?* Suddenly, one of the waitresses from the bar glanced at Willie, their eyes locking, a worried expression on her face. Willie looked grim. "Raheem, every one of you boys! Go over to Fat Dave's home and level it!"

We all rose from our seats, not quite knowing what had happened. I attempted to ask but my words were dismissed with a quick and angry wave of Willie's hand. "This is no time for dumb questions; it is wartime and the order has been given; do you understand?"

"Yes sir!" I exclaimed dubiously.

We all then rushed to the door, then to the street and began our march to Fat Dave's house. The walk was just a mere two and a half blocks down 48th, and his house sat close to the corner behind the Omni nightclub. A quick memory of meeting the NWA rap group there randomly flashed in my mind, but I quickly shook it off and focused on the mission at hand. I could see Fat Dave's house, but something was different about it. At his moment it seemed to have a red glow around it. And as we walked closer, the glow seemed to intensify with each step. We all noticed the glow was engulfing the whole block of 48th and Shattuck. As we stepped into its light, we were transported into another realm. However, this particular realm was a duplicate of our world, and we not only realized that this was the portal but that Fat Dave and his family were Nashar the whole time! We were all stunned.

I told Tommy to run and get reinforcements; he turned and hurried toward the edge of the glow, barely bursting through a thin wall of red. As he faded into our realm, we continued toward the portal. Carlos suddenly grabbed my shoulder and pulled me back, halting our march. Nashar were going in and out of the house by the hundreds. It was incredible that we underestimated the magnitude of their numbers. He said, "yo man we have to wait for the others; there are *far* too many here."

He then points to the old mansion adjacent to the field where our clubhouse had been built. We ran over to the old mansion, hoping to not be seen by anyone. We'd fo' sho be in trouble if we had to fight several Nashar at once with only five of us. We hid in the basement and waited for our people.

By this time Tommy had made it back to the birdcage and informed the San people that the Nashar base was here in this neighborhood - eliciting gasps and looks of surprise and terror. Shaka rose and ordered everybody to suit up and prepare for battle; the whole place erupted in motion, everyone centering themselves with breathing and chants.

The bartender sent out a universal call to arms that summoned more reinforcements. The walls of the birdcage began to dissolve, and it was revealed to Tommy just then that the birdcage bar was actually in fact a portal for the San.

Shaka, Willie, and Crazy J lead the army to the door and with a jerk of shaka's hand, the door burst wide open. Super willy was standing there with a gold ax in his hand. He joins the ranks right behind Crazy J and the others, following them out into the night. we could see the red bubble then had grown into a huge dome-shaped barrier   Shaka bowled his hand and then clapped hands together, the collision creating a thunderous explosion that pushed those in front of the army backward slightly; the entire army took a long deep inhale and on release they stepped forward. The ground shook as the armys feet smashed down on the earth. again a clap, a deep breath, then exhale with the step boom went the march. the nashars could see us coming and they gathered their children and rush them back into fat Dave house but it was too late for anyone to be shielded from the inevitable battle. The san charged the red fortress with war cries the nashars began their charge the red barrier.

The two factions collided right at the edge of the red wall, the violent mix of two clans erupted like a volcanic explosion of bloodshed, brandishing weapons, and light as wizards and warriors used every tactic they had been taught to defend their people. Seeing that the fight was on, Raheem and the rest of the 48th Street Crew had to join in on the fun.

Raheem looked at J-Will and said, "well my friend, this is it. This is the moment of truth, and the moment we have anticipated. Here is the time to make a manifestation of our dreams and goals a reality. At this moment, decide who you will be remembered as. A warrior, a wizard, or not remembered as anything at all...."

We ran out into the ensuing chaos, shouting and swinging and kicking. The strange kids had come out of Fat Dave's house and were headed straight for us, followed by Hsub, who now donned a long black robe and a crown atop his head. We fought fiercely; the wizards waved theirs spells, which collided in the air with that of the Nashar's, creating large explosions of light and energy that entangled together. The residual sparks from these collisions would sprinkle down on to the warriors below. I had conjured a sword and shield to protect me from these flying remnants, and to cut through the enemy the 48th street mob had fought their way to the center of the battle, where Willie, Shaka, and Crazy J had formed a semi-circle around the mind workers who went in and out of the realms fighting on different planes of existence. The Nashars seem to keep coming as we blocked and cut them down. I was growing tired, but the sight of my brothers standing in the void of weakness was enough to keep me going. I wasn't alone in this fight, and everybody had an important role to play.

"Get to the house!" Shaka ordered, and simultaneously the mind warriors floated upward and we began to clear a path for them. I took the lead, cutting Nashars down as if they were thick jungle leaves. At one point I overextended to strike a Nashar but was cut across my shoulder. I fell backward from the pain, and one of the strange kids seized the opportunity to strike me dead. To my relief, a large shield swooped in to cover me, blocking the blow. When the shield was removed, I glanced up to look upon my defender and to my utter bewilderment, it was none other than Mont! The once merciless and terrifying neighborhood bully had actually found it in his heart to join in on the fight. He reached down and picked me up. There was no time for questions and catching up. The Nashar were still all around, trying to kill us. And so, we soldiered on, heading for Fat Dave's house and the Nashar's portal. We marched on, only stopping when the onslaught was too much to move, and once we gained momentum, we inched closer and closer until we reached the front door. As we ascended the winding staircase, we had made it up only three steps when we were bombarded with fire and stones that rained from the windows and roof. We formed a link chain and guided the mind warriors up the flight of steps, but again we were met with another series of attacks, a blanket of arrows flying through the air and lodging themselves into our shields.

Just then, Willie stood up and conjured a sign that created a blow of energy that knocked the Nasher backward; we were able to climb seven more steps to the door which by this time had been closed. Crazy J rushed to the front and conjured a sign that blasted into the door, weakening it but not being able to completely knock it off its hinges. Willie leaped up, conjuring another sign even more powerful than the first, once again blasting into the door and this time it cracked the door frame. It still did not open. I looked toward Shaka, expecting him to finish the job but instead he appointed me to do so. I arose and I knew that at this point I was still doubtful in my abilities, but the confidence the council had in me filled me with courage, and I took a step forward, placing my hands in the ancient form. I took a deep breath and whispered the ancient words down into my hands and then simply pressed forward, seeing the shock wave of my intention sailing through the air and folding the material over. It created a circular hole that expanded in size until it crashed with the greatest of force into the door, knocking off its hinges and exposing the middle room of the house. Without haste, we rushed the chamber and the mind warriors floated to the center. They communicated to us that the portal was down beneath the house. There was no time to waste; we had to reach the portal and destroy it.

Only one thing stood in our way was Hsub, his strange kid henchmen and the Nasher thought assassins. As we made our way under the dual staircase that led to the upper portion of the house, we looked for a way down. There had to be a hidden door, we just had to find it. As we searched the hall for clues and signs of a lever of some sorts, we stumbled our way through the hall, feeling our way since we were blindfolded by the darkness that surrounded us. Our attempts to light the way with sorcery failed as we went deeper into the house. As we made our way, I had time to question Mont about his life after he left 48th street. He explained to me that the woman that he thought was his grandmother was a Nashar witch, and she had taken him from his real parents. The story of his father was real, though it wasn't the police who killed his father, but instead Nashar Warriors. He said, "Over the years my powers grew, and the witch could no longer contain my strength, so she sent me to the other realm to live in a prison." After many years he was able to escape. He lived in the shadows of this world until Shaka had found and rescued him, training him in the RanSan's ways.

I was amazed at his story; he had survived, and I was proud of him. We were going into unknown territory, only guided by the mind warriors who could only give out sparse directions. The directions also only got more vague and uncertain as we went further down into the house. We eventually reached a door that lay in the middle of a small cave; the door had no lock or handle. Once again ,Shaka looked at me and nodding in the direction of the door, I inched toward it, kneeling and contemplating how to open it. I sat there baffled, and fear and doubt began to set in. Even the look of confidence from the others didn't seem to help the growing uneasiness I felt. My mind began to fill with past failures - my weakness in the eyes of bullies, my fear of being myself, and the longing to fit in. And now here I was, on the precipice of failure one more time, struggling to see through it. I began to hear voices that said to turn away, and that I wasn't capable of entering here. They continued to say, *you aren't smart enough to open this door. You are weak, you don't belong, you have no friends, you have no one, you're alone.* The voices grew louder and louder they splashed around my head uncontrollably, but then there was another voice that broke through, and it said "ain't nothing free, but God."

I paused for a while, then grinned slightly. It hit me, because now I understood - God was free and I was one with God, therefore I was free - free of all negativity and self-doubt, and free of all the chains that held me bound. In fact, at that moment I was filled with gratitude. I realized I was here now at the door to salvation for my people; I had already made it, and I was given the opportunity to help them. I just had to take a step forward. I stood up and stepped over the door, a new sense of determination building inside me. I then dropped into the lower chamber, followed by everyone else. We had finally reached the portal.

***

18.

"The World of Make-Believe"

Hsub was there, sitting on a throne made entirely of skulls. We paused. Shaka spoke first. "It's over, Hsub. There is nowhere to go from here."

"But there is!" Hsub shouted viciously. "This is the space where all things are created, or have you forgotten?" He rubbed one of the skulls, which emitted a high-pitched shriek. Then Hsub turned to me. "Do you see this throne?"

I remained silent.

Hsub chuckled. "It's the sum of all doubt and fear that lingers in the San people's minds." He continued, "I've owned them for hundreds of centuries, ever since I came back from that frozen hell the council banished me to. After I trained those like myself into an army, I raided and plundered your strongholds until I reached this throne. There was no doubt and fear then. it was confidence, love, and all the other emotions that the Great San instilled in your people. But once I took hold of the throne those qualities dissipated into the nothingness. The nothingness is where I live and that's where you've come to die.

With his sunken eyes and long, blank face he raised his hand and snapped his long fingers. Suddenly, time stopped, and there was nothingness. No Shaka, Willie, Crazy J, and no San army. There weren't even any Nashar, and no strange kids - just complete nothingness. Again, I felt that I had gone even deeper into the world of emptiness, and I felt alone floating in pure space. I was falling slowly until my feet felt the pressure of the ground beneath them. Only the sound of my breathing told me that I was still alive, but as quickly as they had vanished, my comrades reappeared beside me and I felt a relief wash over me.

However, that burst of relief was short lived when I saw Hsub and some of the strange kids materialize across from us. Hsub spoke in a snarling hiss, "I told you that I would annihilate you and your people, and now the time has come for it to finally manifest!"

Just as I was about to reply there was a voice from my left side - a low rumble that I'd recognize from anywhere. It said, "Shit, you and your people have been trying to annihilate the

San since the council banished you to your icy wasteland?"

"Here and now is the time in which the war will be finalized, and the San people shall be free of your pursuit, you wretched beast!" It was Willie, who had stepped out of the darkness, Shaka and Crazy J behind him. but the mind warriors didnt come to this level they were useless because they could only see the things slightly after they happened, but this was where everything was created. this was the nothingness, the cause of it all. Willie gestured to hsub to join him in the center of the darkness, challenging him.

Hsub was quick to turn his offer down. "You fool! You think I would stoop to the level of a lackey for the council and fight like a peasant? I have my army of children for that." And with a snap of his fingers, the strange kids rushed Willie, attacking him like a pack of ravenous wolves hunting down an elk. I started to help, but Shaka placed his staff in front me. He looked down at me with a grin as I kneeled on one knee, and whispered for me to be patient. I looked on, wanting with every fiber of my being to help my father, but he didn't need my help. He slung the strange kids around every way possible without actually hurting them; he was able to defeat them easily. Hsub sent another wave of kids at him, and this time the second group of Nashar appeared, ambushing him from behind. Just as they were about to grab Willie, Shaka spun his staff around, smacking the wrist of one of the Nashar. It sounded as if a gunshot had gone off. The Nashar screamed in agony. "We won't hurt the children, but those of warrior age shall feel the complete force of our raft!" Shaka then signaled for everyone to start attacking. Bodies all around were now intertwined, locked in individual combat. Willie, who had thrown the kids back repeatedly, had now joined Crazy J in the ass-kicking feast. Shaka walked toward Hsub, but he ordered up more warriors to act as a shield between him and the RanSan elder. Shaka sent a thought to me just then - "now boy, it is your turn to prove your skills."

I took a deep breath to center my mind. I imagined myself as a great warrior, and I could feel my cells reacting to my thoughts and growing and producing more cells by the minute. I felt the energy they gave me, which in turn gave me more confidence in my ability to communicate with them and to know thyself. I floated to my feet and charged the group of strange kids through the air; I began to glow and my movements were fluidlike, flowing in the unknown material of darkness that surrounded us. I could feel the darkness as I punched through it; everything was in slow motion. I saw kicks and punches before they reached me, and I blocked attacks and broke bones as I went. I was able to see myself from my opponent's eyes, and from Willie's and the others' perspectives as well. I could feel everyone, and I realized at that moment I was, in fact, everyone. I looked at Hsub and he shook his head, no! he shouted noooo! he continued, "you can't know thy self!" and as he tried to conjure up more Nashar, I saw it from his eyes, I was in his mind I had become him, hsub dropped his hands to the side then fell to his knees he looked up at me and said you haven't won anything Raheem! this is only the beginning your mind is vast and I can hide out in any part of it. you'll never defeat me or my people we are you and you are us. Hsub let out a scream before dissolving into the darkness.

I stood there in the void while the faces of all my family and friends appeared and disappeared into the nothingness, all the moments of my journey flashing before my eyes. I watched with amazement, filled with the wisdom and understanding of all things. I realized I was Willie Sharp. I had found myself by going into my own mind and defeating my fears and illusions of limitations. Then I started to fade until there was nothing left, save for a smile and complete quiet.

And then there was light! the sound of tires screeching and skidding by my head as I lay in the street. in front of the boys' club, across the from the Omni nightclub on the corner of 48th and Shattuck. I picked myself up and looked around; I stepped out of the street and onto the sidewalk. The streets were empty. I looked down and noticed a one-hundred-dollar bill laying there, creased and soiled from being tossed around by cars driving past. I picked it up and put it in my pocket, I looked up to smile at the sun. I had to get home to mommas chilli. It was Thursday, January 30th, 1986.

THE END

Message from the Author

I got the idea to write this novel when I began to reflect on my life growing up in Oakland. My father was murdered, and I had no idea that this horrible incident would lead to a life of learning from unlikely sources. The older guys in my neighborhood made sure to shield me from the dangers in our area. My aunt had joined a new thought church and she would take me with her on Sundays; she also signed me up for programs that had a powerful impact on my mindset and ultimately my life.

My neighborhood was rife with drugs and crime, but I was able to navigate the pitfalls until my high school years, where at that point I became rebellious and I wanted to see what the streets were all about. My time in the streets was full of danger and death at every turn. For me, it was more of a case study, thinking it was just an experience that would pass. But it was truly my mentors' wisdom and guidance, coupled with the ideology of the church, that is the reason I was able to squeak through that time period without getting involved in illicit activities or going to prison. I feel like it taught me that even in the darkest of situations you can use your intellect and knowledge to move you into a new space and a new life.

When I decided to write this story, I didn't have any experience in story writing, but I knew from my life experience you just start where you're at. So, while at work I would take out my phone and write in the notepad app. Later I would then email the pieces of my story to myself, because not only would my phone's memory be used up quickly, but I wanted to make sure I had a safe place to store it. I remember losing a chapter because I had forgotten to email them, and my phone was stolen. Can you believe this happened twice? Nonetheless, I did what I had to do to keep this story intact, even if it wasn't the most ideal arrangement, because I knew I wanted people to hear my story. So, I kept on writing, through all types of setbacks - working three jobs, writers' block, and plain ole' life stuff.

The character Willie Sharp is a representation of men in the neighborhood that are not recognized within their community for the impact and influence that they have made in the lives of many young boys growing up in the inner-city neighborhoods. I was always taught by the men in my neighborhood that everything starts in the mind and with a positive attitude, you can overcome anything and do everything you set your mind to. It is my goal that hopefully *in these words, young boys or anyone for that matter going through similar hardships will be encouraged to realize their worth and purpose, and utilize their skills to achieve what they want in life.*

-Robert Thurston Hankins, Jr.

CPSIA information can be obtained
at www.ICGtesting.com
Printed in the USA
BVHW081413011020
590077BV00005B/192

9 781947 928381